U.S. Marshal Harry Bailey and the Case of the Deadly Psychologist

RUTHLESS

U.S. Marshal Harry Bailey
and the Case of the Deadly Psychologist

Genre: Crime and Investigation

Author: Minister Larry Montgomery, Sr.

montgomerybusiness@hotmail.com

RUTHLESS

U.S. Marshal Harry Bailey and the Case of the Deadly Psychologist

ISBN: 978-0-9861290-1-8

Published by Emerging Business Group, Inc.

Baldwin, New York.

U.S. Marshal Harry Bailey and the Case of the Deadly Psychologist

**Dedicated to my wife Joyous and
my children for their love and support**

U.S. Marshal Harry Bailey and the Case of the Deadly Psychologist

ABOUT THIS BOOK

Marshal Bailey goes undercover to take down a ruthless psychologist who moonlights as a hit man for a high powered Hedge Fund Manager.

The doctor hypnotizes patients to commit murders to further advance the business of the Banker, once the clients figure out what he's really doing with their money. Once the Banker finishes plundering the client's accounts he has them killed so he can manage their estates. The Banker just keeps folding one client in for another and taking their money to fund his lavish lifestyle and investment losses.

While undercover Marshal Bailey finds himself the target and ultimately the victim of this upscale game of bait and switch when the Banker plunders through Bailey's stock portfolio and then hangs him out to dry for the psychologist to rid him of. But the psychologist finds herself on the list of suspects when the client she uses turns out to be Marshal Bailey's long time partner Marshal Laura McKnight.

When the murder scheme is foiled the murderous psychologist flees the country taking Marshal Bailey and his partner half way around the world to effectuate an arrest warrant after a cold blooded shot out that leaves a hard worker peace officer dead in a hotel lobby.

Follow Marshal Bailey as he breaks his cover to rescue his partner from a coldblooded desperate sociopath of a psychologist hell bent on escaping persecution in *RUTHLESS*.

U.S. Marshal Harry Bailey and the Case of the Deadly Psychologist

ABOUT THE AUTHOR:

Minister Larry Montgomery, Sr., is a retired Banker currently publishing the only online weekly African-American community newspaper on Long Island. Minister Montgomery, Sr. holds a MBA from Hofstra University, Hempstead, New York where he grew up, married and raised three loving children.

Minister Montgomery is a member of Glory Temple Ministries, Inc., Massapequa, New York where under the Pastorship of Senior Pastor Apostle Bishop Ronnie Deadwyler and Executive Pastor Apostle Bishop Dr. Karen Deadwyler, who in obedience to the Father planted the seed of "Scribe" on Minister Montgomery's heart. To that end, Minister Montgomery committed to penning twelve (12) of the Lord's parables under the cover of the life and times of a fictional character named U.S. Marshal Harry Bailey, entitled: U.S. Marshal Harry Bailey and the Parables of Life series.

That was twelve books ago. Since then Minister Montgomery has written four additional fictional short stories entitled; "The Game of Your Life" and "The Way Station-A three part series", "Beyond the Way Station Part II-To Hell for the Holidays", "The Way Station Part III-'The Day After Life'", "2-1-1 Emergency", "Clinical Trials" and a Special Anniversary Edition of U.S. Marshal Harry Bailey entitled: "The CORPORATE KILLINGS" and the Case of the "Deadly Mailman".

He hopes that you enjoy reading this effort as much as you did or will do when reading any of his previous efforts.

Thank you for considering this work and please feel free to pass it on. We hope you find a few moments of relaxation when reading this book and that you look forward to reading our most recent efforts entitled "Criminal Mastermind" an upcoming series entitled: "The Author", part 1, " The Reader", part 2 and "The Publisher", part 3." Followed by "Black Out", "The Inspector (Mentor or Murderer)" and I.P.O. (Inmate Prison Operations). May God to Bless You and Yours!

U.S. Marshal Harry Bailey and the Case of the Deadly Psychologist

TABLE OF CONTENTS

U.S. Marshal Harry Bailey and the Case of the Deadly Psychologist

CHAPTER 1

My Neighbors Keeper

2:00 p.m. Monday, July 14th, Marshal Harry Bailey's journal entry

'It all started some time earlier in the year, just after Mark Reese moved back in with his father, Joe. Joe has been my neighbor for the last five years or so, ever since his wife died of breast cancer. I see Joe down at the mailbox occasionally, nice old guy, you'd never know for a retired fire fighter he had a such a young son. Mark seemed okay to me, I mean I never had a problem with him until today.

I come to find out that the kind, young man has had a history of mental health issues and that his returning home was from some rubber room facility upstate, his father could no longer afford. Joe's social security and his pension were fixed now and all he wanted to do was out live his investment portfolio.

My name Harry, Harry Bailey. I've been a U.S. Marshals for the last 10 years and I'm pretty good at it, so they put me on my first real under cover case last month and I don't know whether I should quit or thank God for the peace and quite. I miss my partner, Marshal Laura McKnight. Laura is cool but once she gets on to something all hell could break out and she is like a

U.S. Marshal Harry Bailey and the Case of the Deadly Psychologist

dog with a bone until she finished it.

Back to Joe and his son Mark and today's unbelievable events. I came in last night on a red eye from Cancun and after a weekend in the son and sand all I wanted to do was sleep, but a package came via FedEx from my broker and I had to sign for it.

Some broker this piece of slim is, Jeffery Foster, mister second tier Wall Street. A hedge fund manager making loans to farm belt colleges looking to build or expand their dormitories to increase student enrollment. The guy is making a ton of loans and the spread on the financing is great but the State Banking Commission has their eye on this guy from every angle. Those are the people who asked the Marshal Service to assist thus I am the undercover agent. No one is sure if this guy Foster is running another punzi scheme or not and its my job to prove it one way or the other.

Anyway back to my neighbor Joe. No sooner did I sign the FedEx receipt then I heard all of this racket coming from down the hall. Joe's three bedroom apartment is next to mines. There is a stairwell between us but our kitchen walls do adjoin. The noise from the yelling and cussing was so loud the FedEx had already called the police when I opened my door to receive his package.

Neighbors had begun opening their doors to see what was going on. And for that to happen in this high rise it had to be serious. We have door men, garage valet's and a ton of security camera's throughout the building and at a thousand dollars a month in maintenance fees on top of a million dollars a unit it should be as quiet as a graveyard around here.

U.S. Marshal Harry Bailey and the Case of the Deadly Psychologist

Before the police could get off of the elevator a bullet tore through Joe's door just missing Mrs. Roberts the next door neighbor across the hall from Joe's apartments; head.

At that point I knew it was going to be a longer day then expected so I grabbed my identification, and my weapon from the foyer desk drawer and made my way down the hall to Joe's place.

Just then the elevator which was set in between my apartment and Joe's door opened, and a team of uniformed officers stepped out. As they pulled their weapons and began to shout at me to drop my weapon, Joe stumbled out of his apartment covered in blood and his son Mark draw down on me from inside the apartment door, just out side of both police officers sight.

My mind started racing, shot and explain later. Is he gonna shot his father? Or is he gonna shot me. God, should I just kill this fool or wound him?

All I knew was what I could see and hear; I got these uniform officers yelling at me, my neighbor Joe stumbling around In between me and his agitated son with a s&w .38 pointed at me, and I'm the only one who can see the entire picture. This could go south in a heart beat, but thank God the FedEx guy was still standing in front of my apartment with his clipboard and he said to the officers, "The guy in the robe is a cop."

That was when the other officer stepped closer and saw the barrel of Mark's gun point at me and his father wobbling back and forth between us. The officer signaled his partner to walk along the near side wall line between Joe's and mine apartments while he trained his weapon at Joe's doorway.

After the longest five seconds in the history of the world Mark backed up and slammed the apartment door closed and started yelling again. Joe hearing the door slam so loud finally tipped over and fell down and I was able to move to the far side of Joe's doorway pushing Mrs. Roberts back inside her apartment and telling her to close the door.

There was silence in the hallway for a moment and I cleared my head. That was when I grabbed Joe by his pants leg and pulled him close behind me, still keeping my weapon trained on the his door.

Joe started to come to himself and the office that was closes to me waved for my attention. After checking Joe I tried to signal to the other officers that he was okay. He hadn't been shot it looked as if he had a nasty gash on the top of his head.

At that point the stairwell door opened and two more uniforms looked into the hallway. The officer closes to them stepped into the doorway and updated them on the situation. Finally I just took charge and yelled out to Mark, "Mark you all right? What's going on? Your father looks like he hit his head. What's going on buddy?"

It was silent for a moment and then Mark babbled something and I said, "Hey buddy you gonna come out here and help me with your father? I can't get him on the elevator by myself." I hovered over Joe for a moment just in case Mark opened the door. I wanted to be in position so he could see me helping his

U.S. Marshal Harry Bailey and the Case of the Deadly Psychologist

father and not see my weapon but be ready just in case he still had his gun.

Mark came to the door and cracked it opened to peak out, and when he did the officer closes to me put his shoulder down and rammed the door so hard it knocked Mark back about four feet and the second officer followed the first one in from behind with his weapon pointed straight ahead. Lucky for Mark the force from the first officer ramming the door open knocked him down and he dropped his gun which slide about 15 feet behind him under the sofa.

The second officer immediately got to his feet as did the first officer and they tackled Mark, pinned him down face down and handcuffed him.'

8:00 a.m. Thursday, July 17th Lobby of Marshal Bailey's Co-Op building

As usual it was another hot and humid July day on 3rd Avenue and I was on my way to see my chief suspect for the first time when my neighbor Joe Reese for the first time since the incident with his son. Joe was standing at the mailbox bank when I stepped off of the elevator.

I spoke and said, "Hello Joe how is your son doing?"

Joe smiled and gave me a great big huge and said, "Harry I thank God you didn't kill him the other day. He has so many problems over the years. Ever since his mother died, God rest her soul, he has been on and off of his meds. His behavior is so sporadic I never knew if he had been taking them of not. He has had these mental issues since birth, but he is my son. The judge asked him if he would go back on his meds and meet with a court appointed doctor before he passed judgment and he agreed; thank God. I don't know what went wrong he has never gotten this bad; a little yelling a little door slamming but never a gun. The Judge told him to see the court appointed psychologist today. Once Mark gets evaluated the judge will decide whether to confine him or not. Harry I appreciate your not shooting him the other day he is all I got."

10:00 a.m. Thursday, July 17th Offices of Blue Mountain Dormitory Funding, 345 Broad Street, Lower Manhattan, NYC Stephen B. Hamilton CEO

When I stepped off of the elevator I was amazed at the style and lavishness of the offices interior. All I could see was smoked glass, black marble floors, large scenic views and grand artwork. The place was very quiet there were only three people sitting in the reception area and one of them was the secretary behind the large glass desk with one telephone and a note pad on it. If her skirt was any shorter or her legs any longer I might have set up a tent in the lobby but I digress.

I walked over to the young woman and introduced myself and asked to see Mr. Hamilton. She smiled and buzzed him. I could see through the smoke glass floor to ceiling windows that made up his office that he was there because there was no one else on the entire floor, everything was open and visible, except the stairwell the restrooms and elevator bank.

When she hung up after introducing me she sent me right in. Now my goal was to make nice, explain to him how I heard of

RUTHLESS

him and why I would like him to handle my investment portfolio. I needed this guy to comfortable with me real quick. The State banking Commission believed they had a strong enough case to shut him down but they felt they needed much more if they were going to put him away for a long time and it was my job to get that evidence.

When I got to his office he stood up and I could see he was a large well dressed man. He walked around from behind his desk to shake my hand and show me to a seat on his sofa that sat next to one of those floor to ceiling windows that over looked Wall Street from this 23rd floor perch. But what struck me as over the top was the very large diamond shaped cufflinks he wore.

I told him that I was a consultant with a pharmaceutical company and did a lot of travelling training new sales representatives and that during my travels I found myself among people who might be interested in working with someone of his caliber here in New York. That was my cover story and he seemed to be very comfortable with it.

Stephen gave me the five minute overview of his business strategy and laid out the successes he had had over the 20 years he'd been in the business. He occasionally dropped a name or two of funds and colleges who had benefited from his service's primarily those historically black colleges and universities that were most publicly familiar; such as Howard University, Tuff University and Morehouse College to name a few. Once he felt that I was completely impressed he went over my statement of network.

U.S. Marshal Harry Bailey and the Case of the Deadly Psychologist

When I handed it to him he looked at it as someone looking for directions to the highway in the middle of farm country. At certain locations he either raised an eye brow or just grunted. After a minute he began his query about my financial strategies and wealth plans.

Everything I said was right from the script the Banking Department had given me. Finally he said, "Look Harry I can tell by your investment experience, and the size of your portfolio you are no novice to this game. I believe I can double your portfolio over the next 36 to 48 months if you just trust me and follow my lead. Now were are going to need you to commit to funding your account upwards of $5,000 a month for the next 24 months. When we have opportunities to partner in a deal we will expect to charge you under our fast track plan, a separate amount of $10,000 to $25,000 depending on the risk and return anticipated. If you would like to cap that activity no problem just let me know. Now Harry I can assure you that over the first 12 months you will be investing like never before. But thereafter you will start to see that the returns will start to flow in, in chucks and as I promised you a few minutes ago we will more than double your $3,000,000.00 portfolio in less than 36 to 48 months. Are you with me?"

Of course I agreed to be with him, he was the mark as they say in the crime and investigation game. Then I turned the tables and asked him a few questions.

I said, "Look Stephen how does this work? If I refer prospective clients to you what is in it for me?"

His response was "Well that would be great but there is no way that I could compensate you for your referrals, which would be illegal." So I said, "I have a number of friends who would like to support these historically black college projects, some have larger portfolio's than me. I mean I won't tell if you don't."

Stephen looked at me and said, "My practice is way more valuable to me than breaking the law. Now if you'll excuse me I have someone waiting."

I got up and started out the door and then he said, "I have an investment consultant that I work with from time to time, I want to refer you to him. Is that okay?"

I responded and said, "I have reached my limit with consultants for this year, thanks anyway."

Then he said, "This is a special kind of consultant he helps people make money from their referrals to professional people like me. You'll like her and if you have as many prospective investors as you say she just might be what you are looking for. Her name is Sharon Romani. I'll have her call you in the morning. Nice meeting you now let's make some money."

10:00 a.m. Thursday, July 17th Offices of Dr. Sharon Romani Clinical Psychologist 336 West 18th Street suite 4, NYC

Mark Reese stood outside the newly remodeled brownstone and when he finally rang the secure lobby door bell for Dr. Romani office he was immediately buzzed in.

It took Mark a couple of minutes to walk up the 8 flights of stairs and he was a little winded when he arrived. Dr. Romani secretary was standing in the doorway waiting for Mark when

U.S. Marshal Harry Bailey and the Case of the Deadly Psychologist

he appeared in the stairwell doorway. She had him fill out a short questionnaire and then she led him into Dr. Romani private office and left. Mark sat and looked around for a few minutes and just when he found himself bored out of his mind he got up to look out of the window and that was when the doctor walked into the room.

While Mark was a tall strapping blonde haired blue eyed hunk of a 24 year old Dr. Romani was a well built 170 lb. full figured 40 year old woman with long jet black hair and a southern draw to die for. She stepped into office with a clipboard in one hand and a cup of coffee in the other. On the clipboard was Mark's court file and medical records.

Dr. Romani spoke and said, "Mark Reese? Please have a sit." Mark sat down in a chair across from her desk and Dr. Romani said, "Wouldn't you feel more comfortable on the sofa?"

Mark got up and walked over to the sofa by the window where he stood and looked out earlier. When he settled down Dr. Romani said, "You been taking your meds?"

Mark responded and said, "Yea the judge said, I gotta or I might wind up in jail if I didn't."

Dr. Romani looked at her clipboard and said, "Which ones are you taking?"

Mark said, "Today I took all of them."

Dr. Romani said, "I asked you a question that was not an answer. Which ones did you take today?"

U.S. Marshal Harry Bailey and the Case of the Deadly Psychologist

Mark looked at her and said, "Whatever they said on the chart. What you can't read or something?"

Dr. Romani stood up and walked to the day and opened it. Then she said, "I asked you a question, now either you answer it or you can leave and take your chances with the Judge, your choice."

Marks sat up slightly and then laid back down and said, "You can say what you want, I told you to look at the chart."

Dr. Romani said, "Fine! Have it your way." Then she walked out of the room and closed the door behind her. As the door was closing she said, "Linda have Jeff and Frank clear my office and send Judge Clarke my bill."

Mark sat up wondering who Jeff and Frank were but he didn't have to wait long to find out. Before he could stand up Jeff walked in the door Dr. Romani had just left from and Frank seemed to appear out of no where, coming in through the doctors private entrance hidden behind the bookcase behind her desk. The two men grabbed Mark up and as Mark pulled to keep from being pulled out the door Dr. Romani left through the two men pulled him towards the private door behind the desk hidden behind the bookcase. When Mark realized what was going on he began to yell out, "Doc. Doc. I'm sorry. I'll talk."

Dr. Romani did not respond and the two men pulled Mark into the back room behind the bookcase over to a large window over looking a fenced in alley 8 stories below. Mark began to panic when the men lifted him up and out of the window. He quickly began screaming for his life. That was when Jeff hit him

U.S. Marshal Harry Bailey and the Case of the Deadly Psychologist

in the stomach so hard it winded him and he could no longer draw enough breath to make a whimper much less an audible screams. As soon as Mark realized the only thing between his head and the pavement 8 stories below was air Dr. Romani called to Jeff and Frank and said, "I think he got the point. Mark did you get the point?"

Marks whimpered a yes and a thank you and the men brought him back in and sat him on his feet.

Then as they led him back to the sofa and sat him down, Dr. Romani said, "Now Mark I want you to remember this episode it was designed to get your attention. What Dr. Romani wants, Dr. Romani gets or no one survives. Is that perfectly clear?"

Mark paused as he tried to pull himself together and Jeff turned around and slapped him on the back of his head he almost passed out, and said, "The Doc asked you a question."

Mark quickly pulled himself together and "Yes, yes. Please don't let him hit me again. Yes. Oh God yes."

Dr. Romani smiled and said, "Jeff will have a seat over there behind my desk while we talk so there will be a smooth flow of questions and timely answers between you and me. The next time we meet I'll just let Jeff ask the questions unless I get the fullest of cooperation from you, Mark is that perfectly clear?"

Mark quickly rubbed his head and said, "Yes mame."

Dr. Romani smiled and said, "Now that's a good boy. Now that I have your attention we can begin."

U.S. Marshal Harry Bailey and the Case of the Deadly Psychologist

When Dr. Romani finished Mark's session she stood up and Jeff went and opened the door. Then he signaled for mark to leave. As Mark quickly got up and walked out the doctors next client was walking in. The two looked at each other and while mark tried not to stir he did remember he was tall, well dressed and wearing a set of the large diamond shaped cufflinks he had ever seen.

4:00 p.m. Thursday, July 17th Starbucks Café across from 26 Federal Plaza the U.S. Marshal Service Regional Office

I was seated on the far side of the right front window of the Starbuck's, the one directly across the street from our office at Federal Plaza when my cellphone rang. Now I didn't recognize the name or the number so at first I thought to just let them leave a message but at the last minute I decided to take the call. Now normally I would have let it go to voicemail since I was waiting for my contact to meet me for our weekly investigation update. But curiosity got the best of me and I answered it, it was a sexy sounding woman named Sharon Romani.

The conversation went like this; she said, "Hello is this Harry Bailey? I am Sharon Romani a friend of Stephen Hamilton your investment advisor. How are you, sir?"

I said, "I'm fine and how are you?"

She said, "I'm well. Thank you, Stephan asked me to get in touch with you in hopes that I might serve as a go between for your referrals to him which would allow both you and I to directly benefit from any referral made to him."

U.S. Marshal Harry Bailey and the Case of the Deadly Psychologist

I acted as if I wasn't clear about what she was talking about while I engaged the voice recorder APP on my iphone. I said, "Can you give me that one more time so I'm clear?"

She said, "Why don't we meet and I can explain it to you slowly."

Now that was a cut I couldn't duck but I took it. I went right back her and said, "No that is alright we can save a lot of time if you just speak into the phone."

She responded and said, "Are you in the City my offices are not far from Stephens we can meet somewhere in between for coffee, my treat. Is tomorrow morning around 9:30 a.m. good for you? There is a nice clean Starbucks on 23st and Lexington I'll be wearing white, all white. Friday's are my late day and Stephen tells me you are worth meeting."

I tried to put it off but before I could clear my throat she came back at me and said, "So it's a date. See at 9:30 sharp ... chow!" And she hung up.

That was when my partner Marshal Laura McKnight stepped into the Starbucks for my debriefing.

Marshal Laura is a smart, resourceful and beautiful law officer. Originally from the Dominican Republic; she and her sister share a Condo in East Harlem. Laura has been in the Marshal Service for over 10 years now she is a former Navy S.P. and a graduate of John Jay College with a degree in Criminal Justice I believe. Did I say beautiful in a professional sort of a way she is, I have to give her credit. Nut from a man to man way, she is really hot.

U.S. Marshal Harry Bailey and the Case of the Deadly Psychologist

She is tall and full figured with long black wavy hair with big brown eyes that could take your breath away if you looked in them too long. Now I have seen her get mad and she can be a handful. Laura has I don't know how many belts in Street Fighting but I have seen her trophy wall and it is impressive.

So anyway Laura sat down and the first thing she said was, "The boss wants this recorded so I'm recording it."

I said, "Come on Laura you gotta give me a chance to get up to speed first. Okay look, I met with the mark, Stephen Hamilton and I have good news and bad news."

Marshal Laura smiled and said, "Speak into the microphone Harry, I'm not going to get in the middle of you and Bert and what he told you to do anymore."

So then I said, "However this guy is working the law he has a sidekick to shield his transactions. I just got a call from her before you walked in, we have a meeting set up for tomorrow morning. That is the good news. The bad news is I'm going to need to make an acceptable referral to this guy probably within 48 hours once I hear how they work. So you my friend are going to need a cover and plenty of cash to back it up."

Sp then she responded and said, "We expected that something like that was going to be needed so what is the bad news?"

I said, "I want it to be you, I think this go between is going to be looking for more than I am willing to go for."

Now Laura is a friend and a great partner and I would never want to screw that up but I knew what she was thinking so I preempted it and said, "Now this is about making her think that there is something between you and me but I want her to first be able to find out that you are a Marshal. Which is something we did not discuss and second I want her to think that you have hoodwinked me into some back room undercover plan. I mean I want her to think that I am a special project of yours and that you are only focused on scamming me. I want to see if I can get her to be my friend like she is a friend to Hamilton. You see?"

I continued and said, "Now Hamilton is ready to add me to his ATM machine at the rate of $10 large a month up to $25 or $50 if I let him. He thinks I just gave him the key my whole $3 million dollar portfolio. So we better be ready to move on him fast. And leveraging his sidekicks loyalty will give us an inside edge one way or another."

U.S. Marshal Harry Bailey and the Case of the Deadly Psychologist

CHAPTER 2

SOMETHING IS WRONG

8:00 p.m. Thursday, July 17th, Midtown Library 3rd Avenue Investment Club Monthly meeting, Room 8A

Seated around the conference table was Joe Reese the club Chairman, Vice Chairman Brenda Moore, Treasurer Alex Winfrey, Secretary Lidia Bruce and investment advisor Donald Romani. The room was packed with over 20 other club members seated around the walls and standing where ever they could. The club Treasurer Alex Winfrey began his report with the following statement: It has come to my attention that among the investment pods we have funded only one needs serious discussion at this time. Of the 10 pods we have funded over the years one has failed to perform and that is the Hedge Fund managed by Stephen Hamilton and Associates, better known as Blue Mountain Dormitory Funding. As many of you may remember this fund specializes in Historically Black College and university Dormitory funding projects which is real estate based mortgage funding. To date we have invested 8 million dollars in anticipation of receiving a 15% to 25% return on the equity funding we made and as of the close of this quarter we have lost almost 5 million dollars due to defaults. We are told that the college dormitory projects we funded the schools have either closed or lost accreditation making them ineligible for matching funding from various government funded programs. The floor is now open for discussion."

Brenda Moore the club Vice Chairwoman stood up and said, "Mr. Chairman I and every other investor in this room are totally disappointed with the performance of this Blue Mountain Hedge Fund and at this point closing our account and cutting our loses is the least of our concerns. I, we want legal action to be taken because I can't see why, that with just a little work this Mr. Hamilton could not have foreseen these schools going under. We understand that there were at least 10 schools in this lot and you mean to tell us that everyone of them has gone into default. That seems very unlikely and very suspicious for such a seasoned fund manager to admit."

Vice Chair Woman Moore went on to say, "Joe, Mr. Chairman, I, we demand a formal independent audit of the funds activities as well as a formal request of the State Department of Securities to investigate this firm. And we expect a formal report back at our next meeting in August."

Chairman Joe Reese raised his hand and said, "Now Brenda no need in getting all in a huff. I too have lost money with that pod and I'm just as fired up as you are. This failure boggles the mind. We put in $8 million dollars hell we could have built our own dormitory with that money and saved the investment commission fees of almost $250,000. Now I'm going to meet with this guy Hamilton first thing in the morning and see how and if we can get our money back."

U.S. Marshal Harry Bailey and the Case of the Deadly Psychologist

That was when the clubs Investment Advisor Donald Romani raised his hand and began to speak.

Donald Romani said, "As you investment advisor I need to advise you that Blue Mountain hedge fund is a licensed investment organization and threatening to sue them without going through the proper channels is just going to waste time and money. Let me make a meeting with Mr. Hamilton and ask him if he could find time to meet with out executive committee in time for our next board meeting. Once we have meet with him and given him a chance to explain what happened then we can present our case to the SEC and the State Department. That is the best way."

Alex Winfrey the club Treasurer stood up and slammed the conference table hard and said, "We didn't have to meet with him and then go to some darn SEC and State Commission or whatever before he took our money why we gotta go through all these hoops to get it back? And first of all as the club Treasurer if you got anything to say to Hamilton I should be with you. I don't want any more secret meetings with people who loss money especially mines."

Chairman Joe Reese stood up and said, "I agree, Alex you make the meeting and invite Donald and when you finish call each of us so we can get together and see where we are before next months meeting."

9:30 a.m. Friday, July 18th, Starbucks 23rd Street and Lexington Avenue

When I walked in and looked around for a woman in white it

U.S. Marshal Harry Bailey and the Case of the Deadly Psychologist

looked as there was a white sale that had exploded into the street in front of Macy's, everyone was wearing something white. But sitting in the back just outside of eye sight was one woman whom God only knows had to be the one I spoke to on the phone. I could by the stare in her eyes this was no woman to be played with. I couldn't tell if I was looking at a black widow or a cold blooded cobra but she was stunning.

When she saw me I knew she knew it was me, she put on a 'Hi! I'm over here smile.' And the glow just pulled me in. I thought if it wasn't her I was going to get to know her one way or another no matter what.

I smiled as I approached stuck out my hand and said, "Ms. Romani I presume?"

She stood up and all I could see was legs and more legs.

She said, "Harry I presume? Please join me."

I sat down and she said, "My, my, my, my aren't you the handsome devil? And just the way I like'em, rich."

I smiled and said, "I'm ok. But you on the other hand, wow!"

She giggled and shyly looked towards the guy behind the counter and mouthed 'Decaf light with sugar'. Then she turned to me and said, "What would you like? Coffee, tea or me?"

I was floored. I almost couldn't contain myself, but I did. I pulled my hands off of the table and placed them in my lap and then I said, "Well I can see I'm out of my league already so why don't

U.S. Marshal Harry Bailey and the Case of the Deadly Psychologist

we just get down to business?"

She said, "How old are you? Don't tell me you afraid of a mature woman? One who knows what they want and gets it?"

I responded and said, "Mature? If you are a day over 38 the coffee is on me."

She laughed out loud and said, "I think we better get down to business before we find ourselves just getting busy right here. Or maybe?"

I said, "Business first, please."

She said, "Okay, fine. Business first and then we will see what happens. Actually I have a very busy day ahead of me so let's make this quick. Stephen tells me you might have some referrals for some of his projects. And in exchange for those referrals you'd like to be compensated, which is understandable. This type of situation comes up all the time and over the years I have been his go to person to work things out."

I said, "His bag man?"

She looked at me with a no nonsense look and said, "I prefer bag woman" then she smiled.

She went on to say, "This is how it works. Any body you believe is interested in investing with Stephen you have them call me directly and have them give your name as their referral. I will then put on my Assistant Broker hat, take their particulars and speak to Stephen. If it is someone he is interested in taking on then I will set up a meeting with them and Stephen. Should

U.S. Marshal Harry Bailey and the Case of the Deadly Psychologist

things go to the next level, a relationship is solidified and an account is opened. I will give you 75% of the calculated commission; the other 25% is mine. The funds will be payable on a gift card for tax reasons. Typically with an investment account funded between one and three million dollars the commission is 6 points or $60 to $180 large. You cut will be 75% or between $45 and $136 large. For deals in excess of these numbers we can negotiate the commission. Now does that work for you?"

I said, "Sounds good, when can we start?"

She responded and said, "Okay! My kind of guy a go getter. We can start as soon as you are ready. Do you have someone in mind?"

I said, "Yes matter of fact but left me talk to them first and get back to you, Okay?"

That was when my cellphone rang and I excused myself to take but she said she had clients waiting as well so she left.

The call was from Marshal Laura she asked me how long was I going to be; she had a crime scene that she thought I should visit. I told her I had just become available; no thanks to her. Then I asked if she could give me a little more information on it and she said, "It maybe relevant to the case and then she had to go.

10:35 a.m. Friday, July 18th, 375 Park Avenue West, apt. 3B

By the time I got there everybody who was anybody was already on the scene so I tracked down Marshal Laura to get an

U.S. Marshal Harry Bailey and the Case of the Deadly Psychologist

update. She introduced me to the lead detective from the 21st Precinct NYPD, a Det. Don Durant and his partner Det. Steward Lake.

Det. Durant was the chatty one but Det. Lake seemed to be the thinker of the team. Det. Durant said, "Your partner here Marshal McKnight said you might want to take this one off of our hands. What we know so far is the victim was shot twice with a s&w .32 revolver. We are in the process of pulling all the surveillance video we can get out hands on. His name was Alexander Winfrey a retired pharmaceutical executive out of Florida. This is his summer apartment, go figure."

I responded to him and said, "Was he robbed? I mean why am I here. Laura?"

Marshal Laura smiled and said, "Mr. Winfrey was the Treasurer for a investment club named the 3rd Avenue Investment Club. It seems Mr. Winfrey here was about to disassociate the 3rd Avenue Investors Club from a Mr. Stephen Hamilton and Associates of the Blue Mountain Dormitory Hedge Fund. The 3rd Avenue Investment Club had just lost about $9 million dollars between some 20 people over a period of four years I believe."

I looked at her and I know she thought I thought she had two heads but I was just wondering how she gets so much information so quickly, but that's Laura. At that point one of the forensic team officers came over and said they had the surveillance video footage cued up waiting for us. So the four of us followed him to the building security office to check them out. When we got there, the first thing you notice was the operation was well set up. I mean for a building that had 8 floors and 4 apartment to each of them not counting the first floor, they had 28 apartments but the security room was set up for six or eight people to work comfortably together. Everything was state of the art, motion detectors, high speed video with sound I was shocked but it made our job a lot easier. So we watched this young white male slip into the building right behind the mail man as if he was delivering a package. He looked legitimate at first glance but when he took the stairwell up you could see he was up to no good. He used the package he had in his hand as a wedge to keep anyone from following upstairs.

Once he got up to the third floor it was easy, some kid waiting for the elevator opened the stairwell door and let him in. He found the apartment quickly and just knocked on the door. I guess the victim was accustom to neighbors stopping by he didn't even ask who was at the door before he opened it and bang, bang it was all over. But then as he was walking out the front lobby door he walked right by the security camera and we had a nice clear shot of his face and the face was familiar. I couldn't believe it, so I didn't say anything in front of the NYPD detectives. I waited until we heard back from their Captain that we could take over the case and then I told Marshal Laura what I thought.

I told her the shooter looked like my neighbors mentally ill son, Mark. She thought I was nuts but I convinced her it was and we took a trip back to the 21st Precinct to wait for the forensic guy's to process the fingerprints on the package the killer left on the stairwell to see if I was correct.

U.S. Marshal Harry Bailey and the Case of the Deadly Psychologist

As soon as we got confirmation on the fingerprints we went directly to Joe Reese's apartment to find out where his son Mark was.

3:45 p.m. Friday, July 18th, outside Joe Reese's apartment

Just as Marshal Laura and I were ready to step off of the elevator Joe Reese was about to get on it. So I stopped him and said, "So Joe how are you today?"

Joe smiled and said, "Oh! I'm just fine and you?"

As we stood in the elevator doorway I kind of blocked his reach to the operating panel and said, "So Joe how is Mark doing these days?"

He responded and said, "Oh he is much better. A little sluggish from his meds but he is coming along good."

I stepped away from the doorway and said, "Joe I was wondering, is Mark in now?"

Joe reached for the elevator panel and said, "Oh! Now? No he had an appointment with his psychologist this morning somewhere down town he won't be back for another hour. He takes his bike for the exercise you know. I can leave a message you asked about him or do you need to talk to him personally?"

At that point I figured I'd take another direction and said, "No that won't be necessary but I would like to take to his doctor do you know the name and address?"

As the elevator doors closed he said, "336 West 18th Street suite

4, a Dr. ..."

I didn't get the name but we had the address so we took the ride to confirm Mark's alibi.

Traffic going down town on a Friday afternoon was relatively light so we made go time. I put the 'Law Enforcement Officer sign in the windshield and we made our way upstairs. It was a very nice super sized brownstone like a doublewide, very posh. When we got to the 4th floor and the elevator door opened right into the waiting room I remember seeing two things. First the high end layout and the large receptionist desk and secondly the floor wall size portrait of Sharon the woman I had coffee with earlier, Stephen Hamilton's bag woman.

I almost missed grabbing Marshal Laura's jacket to stop her from going any further and quickly ushered back on the elevator. When the receptionist noticed that we had stepped back inside the elevator she said, "Can I help you?" And I said, as I turned my back, "Sorry we are on the wrong floor."

Inside the elevator Laura was confused but I explained to her what had just happened and she realized we were lucky not to blow our covers.

So now our next stop was back to Joe Reese's apartment, to pick up Mark. But knowing how things work if Mark we pick up Mark and either Sharon or Hamilton are behind this murder both Laura and I's cover could still be blown if Mark somehow got back on the street. With that in mind we decided to have Det. Durant and Lake pick Mark up and conduct the

U.S. Marshal Harry Bailey and the Case of the Deadly Psychologist interrogation.

7:00 p.m. Friday, July 18th, 336 West 18th Street suite 4, NYC

Sharon didn't even look up from her magazine when Stephen walked into the office. He walked in and strolled over to the sofa by the window and flopped down on and said, "Did you meet with Harry?"

Sharon said, "Yes I did. He seems nice. How much money does he have?"

Stephen took off his shoes and then said, "He is liquid to the tune of low to medium 7 figures. I got the feeling he has more he's just playing it close to the vest."

Sharon said, "I agree. He doesn't sound like he is a risk taker. He is frugal."

Stephen said, "Did he offer you a referral, yet?"

Sharon smiled and said, He will in a day or two. That two is another close to the chest habit. What does he do? How did he make his money?"

Stephen said, "Real estate and family inheritance although I'm not sure if it was grand parents or parents he was a little vague on that."

Then Stephen said, "Things are getting a little tight. I need a couple of new clients like this guy quick, see what you can do. Offer him a bigger cut. Give him an incentive to move quickly will you?"

RUTHLESS

Sharon looked at him and said, "I can see you are a little stressed out. You got many more clients like that Alex and his old geezer investment club?"

Stephen smiled and said, "Those old geezers put up over nine mil. I like old geezers like that."

Sharon said, "So how much did they lose that made them want your head?"

Finally Stephen said, "Come on Doc this stress is killing me. Did you take care of our little problem?"

Sharon slowly put her magazine down and closed it, then she took off her eye glasses and sat back in her high back desk chair and said, "To answer your question, yes and that's going to cost you a little more this time Stephen. My cost have gone up you know?"

Stephen sat up and turned to face her and said, "A little more? How much more, you money hungry bitch?"

Sharon smiled and said, "My name is Dr. Bitch to you and for that the price just went up. I want $250 large in my account by Monday morning."

Stephen stood up and said, "This is highway robbery. I won't pay it. Do you hear me? I won't pay you a dime more than what we agreed upon."

Sharon smiled and pushed back in her chair to get the bottle of cognac from the bookcase behind her desk. Then she reached in her lower desk draw and pulled out a couple of paper cups. She

RUTHLESS

poured a small drink for herself and a large one for Stephen and then she slowly got up while he was still standing and walked over to him and handed it to him. Then she wrapped her arm with the glass in it around his and they both took a sip.

Then she walked back to her desk and kicked her kneels off one by one and sat up on the corner of the desk and slowly lifted her shirk up to show her thigh and the top of her guarder belt.

Stephen took a longer drink and then sat the empty glass on the coffee table in front of the sofa and loosens his neck tie and opened his shirt collar as he approached her. When he stood between her legs he dent over and whispered in her ear and said, "We gonna play doctor patient?"

Sharon reached up, and tugged on his tie and said, "No we are going to play good doctor and bad patient when you answer my question."

Then Stephen took a deep breath and looked up to the ceiling and said, "Yes! Monday, now we play?"

U.S. Marshal Harry Bailey and the Case of the Deadly Psychologist

CHAPTER 3

THE INVESTIGATION

Both Laura and I were waiting in the monitoring booth when Det. Durant and Lake brought Mark Reese in for questioning for the murder of Alex Winfrey earlier that morning. What was curious was the look on Mark's all during the interrogation. He seemed as if he was in a trance or something, not quite himself, unaware of what was going on.

I wanted to shrug it off as shock from the fact that we picked him up so quickly but even that raised a red flag. I mean I asked myself what would be his motive for something like this and this in particular.

When the detectives sat Mark down in the interrogation room and asked him if he wanted a lawyer I asked Laura if she would get Dr. Thomas the services chief psychologist down here just in case my hutch was right, this kid is on something and it ain't alcohol or weed.

Unfortunately by the time Dr. Thomas arrived both Durant and Lake had pretty much exhausted their line of questioning and had gotten nothing but funny looks from the kid. To top that off I had to go downstairs and bring the good doctor up to the interrogation monitoring booth and that required me to walk

RUTHLESS

right in front of Joe Reese, Mark's father, twice.

The first time I was able to put him off but the return trip with the doctor in tow didn't end as well.

The old man accused me of trying to frame his son for no good reason. We couldn't have that because if he walked out with his son with any kind of feelings about me, he or Mark might mention me to the wrong people and my cover would be blown maybe even Laura's as well.

So I had to bring him in on the sting. I told him to wait for me until the interview was finished and then I would bring him up to speed. It was either that or he was going to call a lawyer for his son and we wouldn't get anything and he would probably be out on bail.

When Dr. Thomas got a chance to hear what was going on in the interview he asked if he could examine Mark directly. He said, Mark looked almost comatose even though he was conscious. We had no choice but to agree.

Durant and Lake stepped out of the interview room and joined Laura and I in the monitoring room. After a few minutes and some poking around Dr. Thomas came out and told us that he wanted to take Mark to the ER. He said, "Mark was under some kind of sedative similar to a date rape drug, he was alert but asleep at the same time. I could just see my case going out the window on him but I was warming up to Dr. Romani as the mastermind here.

10:00 a.m. Tuesday, July 22th, Starbuck's 23rd Street and

U.S. Marshal Harry Bailey and the Case of the Deadly Psychologist

Lexington Ave.

I walked in and slipped in line behind Sharon who was reading a magazine while she was waiting to place her order. I bent forward and looked at the cover of the magazine and she said, "Well Mr. Harry how are you? Long time no hear from. What's up?"

I responded and said, "Just got back for a long weekend trip. How are you?"

She responded and said, "I'm fine but I was wondering when are we going to do some business?"

I said, "Right now. I spoke to my friend and I asked them to call you this afternoon. I them you would make the introductions to the investment banker and if things were a go, you'd work out the details. Her name is Laura McKnight. She helped me a few years back with a problem I was having and we have kept in touch. Oh I let her understand that this investment banker was on the high end. You know high risk and high return and she said she was still interested, so we'll see what she does."

Sharon said, "What does she do for a living?"

I said, "She is an independent reorganization consultant. She helps company's and people turn things around."

Sharon smiled and said, "Did she help you turn your business around?"

I said, "Why matter a fact she did. I had a real estate deal that was stuck in the mud and she was able to get it unstuck and

RUTHLESS

moving in the right direction. She was very helpful and smart too. Do you own any real estate?"

Sharon said, "I own a property or two, why?"

I stood back and put up my hands, she sounded as if I was prying into her personal business so I raised my hands and said, "No offense I was just going to warn you that if you did need her services she was pretty pricey, that's all."

Sharon smiled and said, "Sorry I guess I am a little edgy before the first pot of coffee in the morning. That's why I stop here before I go to the office, keeps the staff happy. By the way do you need a ride somewhere?"

I smiled and said, "No my car is outside."

She said, "Where I didn't see you drive up."

I pointed out the front window at the silver 550 SL and said, "That's my baby over there."

She lifted up her sunglasses and squinted and said, "Oh a 2010 baby benz how sweet. Oh! Look you parked right behind 'My baby'" Then she placed her order. I remembered what I parked behind and it wasn't a baby benz it was a big white on white two door Bentley with vanity plates that said, 'My Baby', damn.

4:00 p.m. Tuesday, July 22th, Midtown Marriott Hotel Main Lobby Bar and Grill

Marshal Laura wore her most business like dark blue 2 piece pants suit even though the jacket was a little bulky around her

U.S. Marshal Harry Bailey and the Case of the Deadly Psychologist

glock.

When she arrived to meet with Sharon she was early so she waited at the bar hoping to get a glimpse of her when she arrived. Her instructions were upon arrival to text her and she would have a waiter bring her over.

Laura recognized Sharon from her portrait sitting at the rear of the restaurant close to the restrooms and rear exit back into the main lobby. Sharon was wearing a long brown silk skirt and jacket suite drinking a martini, so she walked over to greet her.

As Laura approached Sharon, Sharon immediately knew who she was and reached out to greet her. Laura sat down and Sharon quickly waved a waiter over and asked Laura what she would like to drink. Laura ordered a white wine and Sharon immediately asked her if she would rather have a champagne but Laura declined.

Sharon began chit chatting about national news and politics' until the drink arrived and then she waited for Laura to begin to sip but Laura didn't. So Sharon asked was there anything wrong and Laura spoke and said, "You know there is something bothering me and I think its you. You know I just can't understand why I need to meet with you as opposed to the gentlemen, Mr. Hamilton, who will be handling my account."

Sharon took a sip of her martini and said, "I can understand that, let me try to answer that this way. I am Mr. Hamilton's chief broker and he meets with no one unless I bring them to him. Now your friend, I believe, Harry assured me that would be the kind of client we at Blue Mountain Brokerage are looking

U.S. Marshal Harry Bailey and the Case of the Deadly Psychologist

for. Are you?"

Laura responded, "As far as I can tell any brokerage firm worth its salt would be looking for a client like me."

Sharon responded, "Let me give you a brief overview of Blue Mountain Dormitory Hedge Fund, we finance historically black and minority colleges and universities construction projects that lead toward greater student population growth and therefore greater revenues and profits. We are looking for clients who have the flexibility of parking at least 7 figures with us for 12 to 48 months and who are looking for aggressive returns in the 30% to 50% range. We require an initial deposit, called your base and fixed monthly deposits that might range from $25,000 to $100,000 each whichever you are comfortable with. And lastly for the more aggressive returns we need to know what you flash point is. That would be how much money we can charge to your account when IPO's make themselves available, the amount you can cover in 30 days or less. These are all secure loans backed by real estate or prepaid construction financing. Can you play in this league?"

Laura took a sip of her wine and said, "I thought this was going to be a challenge. I will make an initial deposit to open my account with you of $1 million dollars. And each year hereafter I will deposit another $1 million dollars for a total of $3 millions if your fund performs as you say. If not I will withdraw one third of the base deposit each year until the account closes. Does that sound reasonable?"

Sharon responded, "Once your account goes below the base amount of $1 million dollars it will be considered inactive and

U.S. Marshal Harry Bailey and the Case of the Deadly Psychologist

ineligible for trading. You will need to cover any loses that occur with in 30 days or the account will be charged and penalty fees may accrue."

Laura sat her glass down in front of her and said, "I understand. So what is the next step?"

Sharon sat back and reached in her briefcase that was under the table and pulled out an application and handed it to Laura.

When Laura reached in her suite jacket to get her checkbook Sharon noticed the but of Laura's glock and said, "Is that a 9 shot or a 16?"

Laura laid down her checkbook and reached for the application to read it and said, "Does it really matter?"

Sharon responded, "What is it that you do for a living anyway?"

Laura said, "Does that really matter?"

Sharon sat quietly and when Laura finished filling out the application she gave her and began to write the deposit check for $1 million dollars she picked up the application and began to examine it. She quickly looked to see what Laura's occupation was and then what her network was. Laura left both her occupation and network information blank. Sharon said, "You left your occupation and network blank. I need to know those answers before I can have this processed."

Laura sat up and said, "I thought Harry told you, I'm an independent business consultant specializing in turnarounds. I come in when all is lost and turn things around. I make a go

RUTHLESS

living at it too."

Sharon looked at Laura and then at the application again and said, "You missed the network figure as well."

Laura said, "I put in as many of my assets and liabilities as I could remember you can do the math can't you, I'm kinda pressed for time."

Then Laura stood up and reached out to hand Sharon her check and say goodbye.

Sharon stood up and took the check and then laid the application on the table and said, "It total's up to $10 million dollars how much of that is liquid?"

Laura smiled and said, "Less the car note and the one mortgage, all of it. Oh! And I took your deposit out of petty cash so the number you have is fine as is. Chow!"

Then she left.

4:00 p.m. Thursday, July 24th, Offices of Blue Mountain Dormitory Funding, 345 Broad Street Lower Manhattan, NYC Stephen B. Hamilton CEO

Sharon walked in just as Stephen had hung up his telephone and sat down in his lap. She gave him a big kiss on the lips and said, "I a new account for you but there is a problem I need to work out first."

Stephen smiled and reached in his top desk drawer and laid a ounce bag of cocaine on it and then pulled out a hundred dollar bill and began to roll it up. He responded and said, "Give me the numbers and the name."

Sharon stood up and walked over to the other side of the desk and grabbed a bottle of tequila and a couple of glasses and sat them on the desk then she went right back to sitting on Stephen lap and said, "This is that referral from your guy Harry, a Laura McKnight, some kind of a business turnaround consultant she calls herself. I think she is a contractor and a very good one. My sources on the street don't know her but they have heard of her, which is surprising. She opened her account with $500 large and I took my fee so you have $450 god funds as of this morning. Did you make good on my account on Tuesday?"

Stephen bent over and took a long sniff of the three lines he craved out and then said, "Yea! Don't you trust me?"

Sharon said, "Yea! I trust you I just wanted know if you remembered with all of this coke you've been doing lately. What's up with this, you hooked?"

Stephen sat back and shook his head as it to loosen up his brain from the effects of the sniff and said, "Did you come over here to annoy me or what? What is you concern with this new account? This Laura? Is she pretty? Or sexy?"

Sharon stood up and went back around the desk and poured her and him a drink and handed it to him and said, "She is very pretty, cocky and smart mouthed as well. And she has a lot of money, over $10 million in liquid assets."

Stephen sat up and leaned forward and said, "Ten million you

U.S. Marshal Harry Bailey and the Case of the Deadly Psychologist

say?"

Then Sharon said, "Either she is a hit man or a cop one or the other. I don't trust her. I think we should just give her, her money back."

Stephen stood up and slammed his fist on his 4 inch thick glass desk and said, "I need that money. I have some losses I need to cover and $450 large is just what the doctor ordered this month. Find out if she is a good guy or a bad one and deal with it, the money stays."

Sharon took a long drink and sat the glass down to pour another drink and said, "I hope you know what you are doing? This could be very messy if she is a cop, you know? Then again maybe she is your guy Harry girl? Did you ever think about what happens when you rip off two lovers?"

Stephen grabbed his drink and walked over to the window over looking Wall Street and said, "We were lovers once and I ripped you off, look what happened to us."

Sharon started to take a sip of her drink and then she paused and responded, "Yea! Look what happened to us."

6:00 pm Thursday, July 24th, Joe and Mark Reese apartment

Joe wasn't too happy to see Laura and I but he let us in anyway. I guess he felt he owed me for not killing his son. So when we sat down in the living room to chat with him and Mark the first thing out of Mark's mouth was, "My lawyer told me not to tell you people anything."

U.S. Marshal Harry Bailey and the Case of the Deadly Psychologist

So I immediately turned my entire body away from him and directed my questions to Joe.

Mark interrupted me and said, "Didn't you hear what I said?"

I looked Joe dead in the eye and said, "Joe I have a few questions for you and since you are not a suspect in any crime that I am aware of would you be kind enough to answer those questions you have knowledge of?"

Joe looked at Mark and said, "For God sakes son the man practically saved your life. What can I help you with Marshal?"

I said, "Who is paying your son's legal bill?"

Joe responded, "Some high priced lawyer from Manhattan was sent to the station to bail Mark out from his therapist office. Why?"

I said, "That was nice of her. What is the therapist name?"

Joe said, "Dr. Sharon Romani, why?"

I said, "Is there any kind of a family or personal tie between you or your son with this Dr. Romani that you would have expected her to pay your legal bill?"

Joe responded, "None that I now of, why?"

I said, "What did Mark tell you happened at his session with Dr. Romani?"

Joe said, "He hasn't said much, really. Just that afterwards he didn't feel himself for a couple of days and that he doesn't have

U.S. Marshal Harry Bailey and the Case of the Deadly Psychologist

any recollection of him getting a gun and shooting anyone, if that is what you are driving at?"

Mark stood up and said, "Dad the lawyer said don't tell them anything."

Joe looked at Mark and said, "He told you that, I don't work for him and he ain't working for me. This man is trying to help us figure out what the heck is going on here, so sit down and listen for once. I'll do all the taking. ...What are you thinking Marshal?"

When Joe asked that question I thought maybe I opened the door to wide but I answered it anyway. I said, "Our guy examined Mark and he believes he was under some kind of a drug at the time. Not a street level but a heavy prescription drug especially mixed up. You see you can hypnotize a person to do things but they will only do things that they would normally do. You have to have some kind of a powerful drug going on to make them do something they won't normally do. And I know Mark is no killer from first hand experience. So we are going with the theory that your Dr. Romani is an important person of interest. But don't tell your lawyer that I need him to do his job and do it well. Is that clear?"

Then Mark said, "I don't remember much about what happened in Dr. Romani's office but I do remember drinking a bottle of water. It tasted funny so I didn't finish it. I think I drank a couple of sips and then put it down."

That was when I asked him if he noticed where the bottle came from, was it from a refrigerator, or did the secretary bring it in

U.S. Marshal Harry Bailey and the Case of the Deadly Psychologist

or what."

Mark responded with, he thought the bottle was on a tray by the sofa he sat on in a ice bucket. But Dr. Romani offered it to me and when I said it tasted funny she reached over and took it and put it on her desk draw. Then she went to her refrigerator and got another one. By then I think I fell asleep and did not fully wake up until yesterday evening."

This is where the conversation got interesting. I guess I said, "Joe you knew the victim right?"

Joe said, "Yes. Alex Winfrey was a member of an investment club I chair."

Then I asked him was there any thing he was working on that might have been a reason for someone to kill him?" And he said, "No."

Then he thought for a moment and said, "No, not really! I don't think. But ...we were about to file suite against one of our investment advisors who lost almost $9 million dollars of our portfolio which was purposively a real estate backed no lost of principal deal. Alex was leading the charge on that one."

I said, "Tell me more" and he did. When he finally told me the name of the investor was Stephen Hamilton I knew we had something. Then he dropped the bombshell.

Joe told us that a similar situation occurred about 5 years ago when the then club chairman went to notify our investment advisor that we weren't happy with the returns and wanted to close our account, he wound up dead as well. Since then we

U.S. Marshal Harry Bailey and the Case of the Deadly Psychologist

started keeping out money in government and municipal bonds only. It wasn't until about three years ago that we went back into the stock market and started investing in equity and hedge funds. They were purportedly very secure especially when real property was backing the deal."

Joe continued and said, "His death is what propelled me into the club chairmanship seat."

That was when Laura asked him who was it that died and how did it happen?"

Joe sat back in his chair and said, "Fred Weeks. Fred was a retired rail road executive. Worked with the motor men's union, some big wig up there; anyway he was hit by a train the night before he was to meet with the advisor. I never trusted that man since then."

I said, "So the death was ruled an accident?"

Joe said, "You damn right it was, no body would listen to us. They just pushed it under the rug."

I said, "What do you mean? The man was hit by a train! Right?"

Joe said, "Fred was deathly afraid of trains, even though he worked for the rail road for over 40 years. He never road one or put himself near a track unless he was driving over it, safely."

So I asked what makes you think it wasn't an accident other than the fact that he was deathly afraid of trains and would only drive across the tracks, safely."

U.S. Marshal Harry Bailey and the Case of the Deadly Psychologist

Joe said, "Fred was hit by a train while standing outside of his Bentley just down the line for a train station that he lived about a mile from back up in Sag Harbor. He had crossed those tracks at least a thousand times in all kinds of weather. There was no reason for him to get out of his car and walk down those tracks while an express train was scheduled to come through there at the same time. He just wouldn't have done it."

I told Joe that I would look into it and see if there was anything more I could find out and then we thanked them and left.

6:00 pm Tuesday, August 29th, Stephen Hamilton Yacht

There was a cool breeze coming across the bow of the boat as Stephen, Frank Bloomberg the brother of Michael Bloomberg the now self appointed King of New York City and Rick Faraday the head of the Construction Trades Union for New York City lounged and drank heavily as the sun was preparing to set.

Frank spoke and the others listened closely because they had all planned for weeks to find themselves in this moment. Frank drunk out in the middle of the Hudson alone with Stephen and Rick.

The two sat quietly as Frank began to outline his brothers plan to upgrade the city sky scrape in the years after he leaves office. Frank boosted that the $100 billion dollar development project would change the list of global real estate developers from the top down and make his brothers name as prominent in history as George Washington or Henry Ford. As he laid out the projects highlights both Stephen and Rick's eye's began to roll back in

U.S. Marshal Harry Bailey and the Case of the Deadly Psychologist

their heads as they counted the money they would make.

Stephen knew Frank was looking for investors who would first line his pockets with consulting fees and then fleece their friends and associates into investing in their relationship with Michael through his brother over the next 50 years of the development project first phase.

Then exactly what both Rick and Stephen were waiting for, the price they would have to pay for Franks favor. Frank told them he would need a $1.5 million consulting fee from Stephen and a $5 million fee from Rick to guaranty them inside access to his brother and his team of developers.

Rick looked at Frank and said, "I'll have a deposit for you first thing next week" and Stephen followed suit and echoed him.

8:00 am Wednesday, August 30th, Stephen Hamilton Office

Stephen looked up from his laptop and there in the doorway Sharon was standing holding a 2 cups of Starbucks coffee. When she saw him looking at her she strolled over to his desk and handed him one cup and then she sat down in a chair in front of his desk and said, "So what is so urgent that you had to see me first thing this morning. I have patients so make it fast."

Stephen stood up and walked over to the window and looked out over Wall Street as he spoke. He said as he sipped on his coffee, "You know I was just privy to a conversation that is going to change how the world will look at New York City through the next millennium. And I need to put my hands on $1.5 mil by this time next week."

U.S. Marshal Harry Bailey and the Case of the Deadly Psychologist

Sharon smiled and said, "$1.5 mil is that all?"

In a frustrated voice Stephen snapped back and said, "This is an opportunity of a life time. The players are in place the idea is solid and the politics could not be better but I'm short on cash. Can you believe it?"

Sharon then looked confused and said, "You clients have money ask them."

Stephen turned around to face her and smiled and said, "My clients funds are tied up cover my client's dividends and losses. The two new accounts you brought in last month is all I have available and I'll still be short."

Sharon said, "What are you gonna need?"

Stephen thought for a moment and then he said, "Bailey has deposited $200,000 over the two months, your girl Laura has put up what? $450,000. I need $1.5 mil so that makes me $850,000 short."

Sharon said, "Is that all you can access?"

Stephen rushed over to his laptop and said, "Let me check one other account, hold on...here it is... I got another $350,000 from an account death policy coming in today but I need $50 of that for expenses so I'm still short half a million."

Sharon said, "Where is that $350 death policy coming from? Who died?"

Stephen said, "Oh How quickly we forget, our friend Alex

Winfrey. You know the old guy you had taken care of last month, his policy."

Sharon said, "Aren't you the executor of his estate as well? I'm sure he had other assets."

Stephen said, "No his wife is the executor I should have checked before I let you take care of him if we had gotten them both at the same time then it would have been me as the executor and their two adult kids. I know he had several pieces of property worth millions in a fire sale. But that is water under the bridge now, I still need $500,000."

Sharon said, "I can through that in but it will cost you."

Stephen walked over to her and sat down next to her and said, "Can you put it up by Friday?"

Sharon said, "Hold on, not so fast. What is in it for me?"

Stephen placed his hand on her upper thigh and said, "A warm and fuzzy feeling?"

Sharon smiled and stood up and as she walked towards the window to look out she said, "Half share. A half share of your share is what I want. And tell me everything you know so far; everything, who, what, where and when. I want names and phone numbers as well."

Stephen responded and said, "A share cost $1.5 mil and you want to buy a half share for $500,000 that is some discount. And you want to what participate too?"

Sharon smiled and said, "You don't have to take the money you know."

Stephen said, "When we do this you are going to have to deal with our guy Harry and his friend Laura, you know that, right?"

Then Sharon said, "Well I can take care of those two but my fee is still the same, $100,000 each payable 24 hours after the job. How are you gonna come up with that?"

Stephen said, "I still have access to Alex Winfrey's power of attorney I'll come up with the cash in time, not to worry."

Sharon stood and walked towards the door and said, "Who me worry? That ain't gonna happen. I'll have the cash on Friday morning you set up the meeting with the one who is gonna make you and me partners and I'll give him my share."

Stephen said, "Oh! So now you don't trust me?"

Sharon opened the door and stepped out and as she pulled the door closed she said, "Hell no, I don't trust you, but you pay on time" then she closed the door behind her.

4:00 pm Thursday, August 31st, Joe Reese Apartment

Mark walked into the apartment just as Joe was finishing up preparing to leave and said, "Pop I'm home. They dropped the case. They said, "There was insufficient evidence that it was me on the video and my alibi was solid. The lawyer told me that double jeopardy had attached so they couldn't come after me again. Man that was some mess."

Joe said, "They dropped it? I thought this was a preliminary hearing."

Mark said, "It was but my lawyer seemed to have them on the ropes and was arguing back and forth. They mist have went into chambers three times before the Judge dismissed the case. I didn't know what was going on. But he tell me I had to continue to see my therapist for the other case."

Now Joe was ready to leave for his regular monthly investment club meeting when the phone rang, it was Helen Winfrey.

Helen asked Joe if he knew anything about the life insurance policy the club held on its members. Joe responded that the investment advisor would have all of that information and then he asked why.

Helen said, she was speaking to her attorney who told her that Alex did not have a policy covering his life with the investment club it was with the investment advisor directly. Which meant she could not even share in it and she was trying to put her retirement plan together. But more importantly she said she wanted to make the club aware of this, because it seems as though the cost of maintaining the policy was coming directly out of Alex's investment account. She said it was like Alex gifted the investment advisor several hundred thousand dollars just for doing a pour job.

Joe said, he would look into it and let the others know. Then he told her that there had been a U.S. Marshal, a couple of them going around asking questions about Alex's death and the investment advisor and he would also let him know what she

U.S. Marshal Harry Bailey and the Case of the Deadly Psychologist

had just told him. Then Joe called me and filled me in.

4:00 pm Thursday, August 31st, The Carlton Restaurant on the Green, Eisenhower Park Nassau County, NY Cocktail Lounge

I was seated at the bar when someone taped me on the shoulder and said, "Fancy meeting you here?" When I turned and looked I almost fell off my stool, it was Sharon.

I asked her what in the hell brought her there and she said, "You aren't the only golfer who knows about this place. May I join you?"

Before I say a word she slowly sat down on the stool next to me and crossed her legs. I had to say that I was quiet impressed by her demeanor and attire. She wore a light colored almost off white and beige pair of knee high shorts and a very conservative tank top. Her hair was pulled back which made her look even more conservative and cute. Before I could say anything she reached in her pocket and handed me a check. When I looked at it, it was for $45,000. I almost dropped it but I had to keep up my image so I just said, "I see you do keep your word. This is for Laura's account?"

She said, "Yes." And then she said, "I have a question for you, what is it between you and this Laura? Are you two a thing?"

Immediately I knew where this was going and I knew this could make or break this relationship so I had to think fast. I just smiled and said, "Why you so interested in my relationships?"

She said, "I just like to keep my business and my clients in their

U.S. Marshal Harry Bailey and the Case of the Deadly Psychologist

rightful lanes."

I took a chance and said exactly what was on my mind. I said, "A fine looking woman like you, good looking, well off, in a position to earn a good living what you want with a player like me? You know how this is gonna play out so why even open the door?"

She thought for a minute and then she said, "Are you gay?"

I almost fell out laughing and then I said, "Are you crazy?"

Then she almost fell out laughing. When we finished laughing she said, "I'm a big girl. I know what I'm doing. You game?"

She had me there, so I said, "I'm sorry I don't mix business with pleasure. But thanks for considering me I am very flattered."

She bit her lip for a second then she uncrossed her legs stood up and walked away.

2:00 pm Friday, September 1st, Dr. Romani Office

Mark Reese sat up on the sofa and Dr. Romani said, "Now Mark remember when your cellphone rings on Monday morning you are to go into the kitchen over to the pantry and drill a 1" hole 12 inches straight through. Then disconnect the gas line to the stove then get the small hose out of your backpack and attach it to the gas line and stick the other end of the hose through the hole. Don't forget the chewing gum; use it to seal the hose in the hole in the wall. Then when your cellphone rings the second time leave your apartment and go down the hall to your neighbor's apartment and knock on the door. When he opens the door pull out your cigarette and say, 'Excuse me, I just

U.S. Marshal Harry Bailey and the Case of the Deadly Psychologist

locked myself out of my apartment can I get a light until the super arrives?' Then wait for him to bring you a light and light it."

Dr. Romani continued and said, "Now when I snap my fingers you will awake, refreshed and relaxed, happy." Then she snapped her fingers and Mark opened his already opened eyes and smiled.

No sooner did Mark lave the doctors office did Stephen Hamilton arrive. Stephen walked in Dr. Romani office just as she was finishing up audio taping her notes from Mark Reese session.

Stephen walked in and immediately apologized for the intrusion as he sat down at her desk. Sharon looked up as he sat down and said, "I thought we were on 4:00 pm?"

Stephen said, "We are just wanted to make sure there were not going to be any surprises. You have the cash?"

Dr. Romani said, "Of course I do. But I am glad you are early we have a problem."

Stephen said, "Yea! What is it now?"

Dr. Romani said, "That last account I sent you. The Laura McKnight account! She is a U.S. Marshal. One of my body guards recognized her at the restaurant. He wasn't sure but after he checked around he verified it. What do you want to do?"

Stephen almost in a panic said, "What can we do? I have already

U.S. Marshal Harry Bailey and the Case of the Deadly Psychologist

charged the cash from the account and Frank should be here any minute, now."

Dr. Romani smiled and said, "I could take care of her for you. You got one of those automatic account insurance policy on her right? So you can afford to pay me."

Stephen said, "I thought you said she had a excessive amount of liquid assets for a working girl. I thought you said she was a contract killer for hire or something like that?"

Dr. Romani smiled and said, "She maybe. I'll check her out, otherwise I'll just get rid of her. Okay?"

U.S. Marshal Harry Bailey and the Case of the Deadly Psychologist

CHAPTER 4

THE STRATEGY

5:00 am Saturday, September 2nd, Outside Marshal Bailey's apartment

My work cellphone rang and woke me up, it was Laura. She said she was outside in the hallway knocking on my door it was an emergency, so I got up and opened the front door. When the door opened Laura grabbed me by the arm and pulled me into the hallway with only my bathrobe on. When I realized what had just happened I looked around and saw several other Marshal's including my boss and a boom squad team standing at the ready. The crowd hustled me into the elevator and as the elevator doors closed I could see the boom squad hurry into my apartment.

My boss Supervising Marshal Bert Cooke began to explain as the elevator descended to the first floor. He said, "They had on good authority that a gas boom was about to be detonated in my apartment."

He went on to tell me that the surveillance team watching Dr. Romani was alerted to the attempt on my life around 5:00 pm earlier in the evening but the message didn't get to him until 4:00 am.

Now how in the hell that happened I don't know and Marshal Cooke assured me that he would personally look into that

RUTHLESS

himself.

When we got downstairs we walked over to our mobile command center and started to discuss our next move.

We all agreed that in order to solidify a case for the attempted assassination of a Federal Peace Officer we might have to let this scheme play out the concern was how to assure everyone's safety. The boom team leader came up with a brilliant idea. He suggested that we could use one of his team members to pose as a housekeeper; let Mark make contact when he is ready and have an explosive blanket hidden behind the apartment door to cover herself with when he ignites the device. After much discussion the plan was agreed to and implemented.

Around 8:00 am, as Marshal Laura, my boss and I watched from the mobile command center via a couple of well placed video cameras in the hallway. Mark left his apartment to knock on my apartment door three times before he actually knocked.

It seemed as though he forgot a key piece of the puzzle two times before he was fully prepared to complete the mission. When he finally had everything, his cigarette, his backpack and his storyline straight he knocked and when the boom squad decoy opened the door he was thrown for a loop at first but he went through with the plan as given to him.

When Mark explained why he was knocking on the door so early and asked for a light the decoy responded and said, "Wait here I will get you a light. Mr. Bailey is not home but you can come back later." Then he closed the door slowing and after a minute returned with a book of matches. As he closed the front door he

U.S. Marshal Harry Bailey and the Case of the Deadly Psychologist

quickly got under the explosive device protection blanket. Mark struggled with the book of matches for a second and when he caught a good strike my kitchen went up like a barrel of firecrackers but with little or no real damage or destruction. The kitchen pantry was gone but there was no fire and no other collateral damage since the gas was actually turned off in both Joe's and my apartments.

What was most interesting was when we picked Mark up off the floor he didn't know anything about what had just happened. We brought him downtown to interrogate him and have him monitored by another court appointed psychologist for a couple of days. What was good to know was that if anyone should hypnotize someone a better hypnotist can undo it.

The fairest wheel continued to grind down even as we debriefed and dehypnotized Mark, Laura was the next tool to be used.

4:00 pm Saturday, September 2nd, Belleview Medical Center 7th Floor Evaluation Ward

Visiting hours had just ended for the evaluation ward and Joe Reese was walking back to his car, which he had parked in the rear of the rear parking lot. As he got in and sat down behind the steering wheel of his car he realized he still had the visitors pass he received from the front desk guard to get upstairs and see Mark, so he pulled it off and dropped it on the ground just outside of the drivers door.

When Joe pulled out of the parking spot a medium sized man walked over to the spot where Joe was parked and picked up

U.S. Marshal Harry Bailey and the Case of the Deadly Psychologist

Joe's visitors pass and walked away with it.

The man walked back around the building to the doctor's parking lot and as he walked past a dark colored Lincoln continental he placed the visitors pass in the drivers side window jam and walked away.

When the man was out of sight a rather large muscular Italian man wearing a stet scope and a white doctors hospital jacket, got out of that car, grabbed the visitors pass and walked into the hospital front entrance.

As he walked through the hospital lobby to the rear elevator bank no one gave him a second look. Then he got on an elevator and rode up to the 7th floor where he was greeted by a hospital guard. The guard looked up from his newspaper for less than a second and said, "Doc you must be new visitor hours ended about 5 minutes ago but I guess it will be okay?" Then he waved him to enter in.

The man grabbed a patient clipboard from one of the room doors in the hallway on his way down the corridor. As soon as he turned the corner to the secured wing he saw two NYPD officers standing and talking outside the room at the end of the corridor.

The officers glanced at him and continued to talk until they realized his destination was the room they were guarding. One officer was seated and the other was standing and talking to him with one eye on the officer he was talking to and the other on the man walking towards them.

U.S. Marshal Harry Bailey and the Case of the Deadly Psychologist

As soon as the man passed the last room on the corridor before the room they were guarding the officer who was standing and talking, turned and said, "Can I help you Doc?"

With that the man pushed the officer who had stepped towards him into the lap of the seated officer and held him down as he pulled a s&w .38 with a silencer on the barrel from the back of his pants belt and put it to the officers head and shot him. Then he shot the second officer in the face. When the two men fell against the wall he shot both of them two more times in the chest.

Then he opened the unlocked room door and stepped inside holding the gun behind his back.

Mark sat up in his bed and said, "Where is Dr. Keller?"

The man slowly walked towards Mark who was about 15 feet away from the door near the window over looking the rear parking lot.

As the man slowly approached Mark, Mark noticed the blood splatter on the front of his jacket and started to recoil. The man pulled the gun from behind his back and stepped up to Mark and pressed it against his head and pulled the trigger, twice. As Mark fell between the bed and the window the man pulled off the white coat he had on and placed the gun in his pocket and turned and walked out of the room.

4:00 pm Saturday, September 2nd, Marshal's Regional Office

Here is where things got hectic and crazy. After Mark was committed for observation my boss Senior Marshal Bert Cooke

U.S. Marshal Harry Bailey and the Case of the Deadly Psychologist

called everyone in for a strategy update meeting.

Marshal Cooke is a brilliant investigator and a world class interrogator but it is hard to understand what he is saying sometimes because of his heavy Jamaican accent. He is highly respected but sometimes it is hard to know when he is being sarcastic, mean, or just plain witty unless you really know him.

Laura and I were sitting in his office waiting for this strategy update meeting when her cellphone rang and she stepped out to take the call. Bert walked in right behind her and asked me why she was so disrespectful which caught me by surprise but before I could respond he said, "Oh! That's right she works for you Harry."

Laura seemed to be tied up so Bert and I went over the case to date. At this point we had Mark dead to rights on a murder and an attempted murder but we could not fully tie Dr. Romani to either charges. We needed a witness and Mark was under hypnotist so he would not be as reliable as the DA would like.

The surveillance team leader reported that there were some audio and video tapes available from there end but the full extent of the case could be gleamed from the patient tapes Romani kept hidden in her office which would require a search warrant and our revealing that she was a target of an investigation. So it was decided if we were going to go for that we better be ready to close the case. It was decided to pick Mark up and arrest him for the murder and attempted murder and see if Romani will try and destroy the evidence. As far as Hamilton was concerned we were going to need set up a wiretap on him as well just in case we need more to tie him and

U.S. Marshal Harry Bailey and the Case of the Deadly Psychologist

Romani together in a full conspiracy charge.

No sooner did Laura come back into the office then my cellphone rang, it was Romani. When I stepped out into the hall to take the call Sharon asked if we could meet. She said, she had just heard that there was an attempt on my life and that the key suspect was my neighbor Mark Reese.

This perplexed me because I didn't know she knew Mark was my neighbor. So I assured her I knew little about the situation. I said I was on the road for the last 24 hours travelling to Boston on business but I was on my way back to New York and would meet her around midnight at the Downtown Marriott. She told me it would be better if we meet at her New York apartment which was upstairs from her offices downtown. I agreed.

By the time I got back inside the office all hell was breaking loose, everyone was preparing to rush out. Laura grabbed my arm and said, "Harry guess what?"

I said, "What?"

Then Laura said, "Mark was found dead and the two officers guarding him had been shot and killed." Marshal Cooke rode with us to Belleview Medical Center to take charge of the crime scene.

On our way over to the hospital Laura filled me in on her conversation with Dr. Romani.

She said, Sharon wanted to contract her services. She said, Sharon had somehow, did some checking and found out that she worked for the Marshal Service but was available for hire.

She said, Sharon gloated that she figured that out based on my net worth. Then Laura said, "Of course that just validated how good an alias the service had created for her. Then she said, Sharon would pay her on performance, twice her normal rate. Meaning that she would provide a phone a location where to meet the target at and upon proof of death she would wire the fee. She said Sharon said she was willing to pay a premium because it was such short notice as well. Then Laura told me that she wasn't comfortable with the way Sharon said she would set the meeting up with the mark. Laura said, she just didn't have a good feeling about the whole thing and she wanted to know if I thought she should opt out. I told her we have come too far to back down now. I said just keep in touch and we'll work everything out.

Then Laura said, "I'm really not comfortable with this. I'm going to call and meet with her first thing tomorrow; get a retainer upfront, find out who she wants dead and then make a decision."

I said, "Not a problem if that is how you feel. I have a meeting with her later this evening so we'll see what happens."

Then Laura said, "Are we going to arrest her tonight?"

I said, "No, not tonight she may have something incriminating to help us tie in Hamilton or who killed Mark and his guards. Let's put an additional surveillance team on her, I think that after today's events we can fully justify that."

6:00 pm Belleview Medical Center Observation Ward Crime

U.S. Marshal Harry Bailey and the Case of the Deadly Psychologist

Scene

By the time we arrived the detectives on the scene seemed to have everything under control. Where we felt we should best spend our time was in the security center going over the security tapes and bingo we got lucky. The suspect must have checked the place out in advance, he knew where the security cameras were and just how to look natural while avoiding them. But we did catch a break one of the front parking lot cameras had been purposely moved into a new position the night before and we caught a glimpse of the car he was driving and a partial plate number.

We headed back to the office and wanted for the investigative reports to begin to roll in. first the crime scene reports from the on scene detectives came in. But they provided little or no information except for the type of gun that was used; an s&w .38 with a silencer.

There was little to go on from the ballistics report and the forensic report but the DMV report was promising. Of the number of dark blue Lincoln continental in the down state area with NY plates carrying the call letters TVE and three digits there were only 10 registered as operating. We took a look at the registered owners list and saw three names that rang bells, but the one that seemed to have the most promise was registered to Dr. S. Romani residing at Dr. Sharon Romani Clinical Psychologist 336 West 18th Street suite 4, NYC. I suggested the detectives in charge make a house call on the vehicles owner while I got ready to make my midnight meeting with Sharon. The crime scene detectives got their warrants to search and

U.S. Marshal Harry Bailey and the Case of the Deadly Psychologist

examine the car while I made my way downtown to see the doctor.

12:00 a.m. Dr. Romani's Office

I rang the apartment bell on the downstairs entrance door and Sharon immediately buzzed me in. Once inside the building lobby area I took the elevator upstairs to the fourth floor but the rear elevator door opened directly into her apartment's front foyer. With all of the high end flooring and finishes I thought I was a home and garden catalog. This had to be a million dollar apartment. I could see just from the foyer that she had a 3 bedroom, 3 bath layout. Sharon quickly accosted me wearing a floor length white silk robe and pajamas to match carrying a dry martini for me. When I passed on the drink I could see she was very disappointed but not surprised.

We walked into the living room and sat on opposite ends of the sofa. I could see she wasn't happy about that either, so I just got to the point and said, "Okay I'm here! What was so urgent?"

She said, "Look I am sure the police are going to be all over everyone I ever met concerning the events of this morning. Have they questioned you, yet?"

I said, "No. I literally drove directly here from Boston. I have several properties up there that I'm trying to sell and the lawyers tied me all day. My door man tells me the place is a mess but no where as bad as it could have been. So you believe one of your clients is responsible for this?"

Sharon sat back and took a sip of her drink then sat the glass down on the coffee table. Then she sat up and said, "I think the young man they should be looking is one of my recently assigned patients. I know he told me he had some issues with his neighbor. Something about black people moving in and taking over or some such nonsense. I didn't really tie him to you until I heard what had happened in the news. I used to own a Co-Op across the street from yours so I recognized the address from your brokerage account application. I don't think I got a change to mention it to you but with the booming and everything today it all just clicked."

She continued and said, "I just wanted to speak to you first so if and when the press got a hold of the story you wouldn't feel slighted."

I played along and asked, "What kind of threats did he make? Do you have him on tape or something?"

Sharon looked at me and then she said, "Why would you ask if I had his comments on tape?"

I said, "Most doctors I know nowadays record everything for insurance purposes, don't you?"

She sat back and smiled and said, "I keep appropriate client records of each session. Don't worry I covered my ass."

I said, "Oh! Excuse me then. But why the late night meeting if everything is copasetic?"

She stood up and walked over to where I was sitting and reached around the back of my neck to caress my ear and said, "I like you Harry Bailey. I was concerned that something might

U.S. Marshal Harry Bailey and the Case of the Deadly Psychologist

happen to you and I would have missed the chance to have at least made my feelings clear to you. Do you care for me, Harry Bailey?"

I looked at her as if I was looking straight through her and said, "I think our business is done her, don't you?"

She stepped back as if a woman scorned and said, "You are right Mr. Harry Bailey our business is done for tonight. You may leave. I just thought it was the right thing to do, to tell you that I didn't know my client was seriously interested in killing you for whatever reason. I have a long day planned for tomorrow but I would like to invite you to dinner at my estate on Long Island. I have a place in the Hamptons. I am having a few guests over, real estate developers you may or may not know and I thought we could maybe do a little more business should I expect you? Dinner will be served at 7:00 p.m. sharp. In case you are interested, dress is casual and feel free to bring your check book. These are the kind of people, who rather act than talk, if you are interested in that kind?"

7:30 a.m. the next morning Monday, September 4th,

Sharon was seated on a bench near the far corner of Park Row and Broadway after her third run around City Hall when Marshal Laura McKnight walked up and sat down next to her. Sharon was startled by contained herself. She smiled and said, "Fancy meeting you here. Come here often?"

Laura smiled and said, "Only when there is money to be made. I wanted to follow up on our conversation the other night and I thought a face to face would be best. Now this is how I work.

RUTHLESS

U.S. Marshal Harry Bailey and the Case of the Deadly Psychologist

First I let my clients know that this is serious business and I take my business very seriously. All I have is my reputation and the work I do to solve the problems you face comes with a price. I don't do rush jobs, but in your case since you are willing to pay the premium I am willing to consider it. The cost is $100,000.00 half upfront and half 24 hours after proof of completion. Not a minute longer or I go into collection mode. And collection mode isn't a pretty thing, trust me. With that said, do we still have a deal?"

Sharon smiled and said, "I'm still listening."

Then Laura said, "Name, time and location of target?"

Sharon said, "I thought you said, you required a deposit of half up front?"

Laura responded, "We're still talking so I am sure you will comply with that detail as soon as we finish here. Unless to carry $50 large around in your fannie pack there?"

Sharon said, "That would be a little to bulky wouldn't it? Anyway the marks name is Joe. Joe Reese. The time is 7:20 p.m. this evening. The location is 35 Clear View Drive, Sag Harbor. If at all possible please take care of this matter in the driveway. He will be driving a silver SL550 convertible."

Laura thought for a moment and then said, "Do you have a photo or will he be your only guest?"

Sharon said, "He will be the only one arriving between 7:15 pm and 7:45 pm, everyone else will be there at 6:00 pm sharp. They all know how annul I am about being late. Now if you'll meet me right here at 11:00 a.m. I will have the cash for you and this phase of our business will be complete; If you'll excuse me?"

Laura stood up as did Sharon and said, "I'll be sitting here at 11:00 am don't be late." And she walked away.

11:00 a.m. Park Row and Broadway Bench

Laura parked in the pay to park garage three blocks from the mornings meeting place and slowly walked to the bench. She timed it just right so that she would be literally sitting down on the same bench her and Sharon sat on exactly two and a half hours earlier. When she arrived and sat down a white on white Bentley pulled up and let down the drivers window. When Laura looked to see who was driving Sharon looked over her shoulder at Laura and pulled down her sunglasses and said, "I'm here! Am I early?"

Laura stood up and stepped over to the car door and said, "I would not have waited a minute longer."

Sharon handed Laura an envelope with $50,000 in cash in it, a picture of Harry seated in his Mercedes and said, "Remember take care of this between 7:15 p.m. and 7:30 p.m."

Laura stood up from the driver's side window and said, "24 hours after proof of life the balance will be due. Or the next time you see me it will be the collection call you will never forget." Then she stepped back and walked away.

Later that morning 12:00 noon, 26 Federal Plaza U.S. Marshal Regional Office

U.S. Marshal Harry Bailey and the Case of the Deadly Psychologist

When Marshal Cooke sat back in his desk chair as he looked at the photo Marshal Laura handed him of me in my car he said, "Harry is this yours or the departments?"

I smiled and said, "Boss you know that is my car. It looks like she had someone take it the other night when I stopped at her apartment and she tried to make me believe she was looking out for my best interest in the Mark Reese murder. This is one sick woman. She is probably looking to have Laura kill me and then set her up. She has no intentions of paying the other half of that money."

Then Bert said, "Laura what do you think? Should we pick her now of wait until the trap is sprung?"

Marshal Laura said, exactly what I trained her to say, "Let's get this fool off the street now and save the man hours, boss."

I know her like a book. But when the boss asked me I said, exactly what I know he would have said. I said, "Spring the trap and then drag them all in at the same time. Split them up and see who's ready to make a deal and give up the rest of them. Case made on confession and case closed with them having no where to run but point fingers at each other."

The Boss laughed and said, "Harry you know me to well. I got to change up a little you might be wanting my job soon."

We all laughed and then he surprised me and said, "I want you two to send a team of detectives to Joe Reese's apartment just in case and then go to this woman's house and pick her up at 7:00 p.m. We have her payment, we have her on video making

U.S. Marshal Harry Bailey and the Case of the Deadly Psychologist

the deal let's just wrap this up."

I said, "What about her co-conspirator Hamilton?"

The boss said, "Let her point the finger at him as the reason why she did what she did. Give the DA a chance to do her job will you? We got other cases piling up around here, get this thing closed tonight."

5:45 p.m. Monday, September 4th 35 Clear View Drive, Sag Harbor

Sharon pulled into the driveway and parked right behind the chauffeured limousine that was already parked there. When she got to the front door the butler opened it before she could even ring the bell and said, "Welcome Dr. Romani all of the guest are waiting for you in the study."

When Sharon walked into the great room which doubled as a study and guest room Stephen Hamilton stood up and said, "And her she is Dr. Sharon Romani glad you could make it on such short notice. You remember Frank Bloomberg from last week, right? I asked him to join us this afternoon because something has come up that I knew he could be of help with, please have a seat."

Sharon shook Franks hand as she sat down on the sofa across from him and Stephen. Stephen asked if he anyone wanted a drink, and Sharon asked for a dry martini as did Frank. The butler made the drinks and Stephen sent him away.

After some small talk Frank looked at his watch and said, "Stephen I don't want to be a stick in the mud but I do have several other stops to make before I fly out this evening can we get started?"

Stephen smiled and said, "Yes. The reason Sharon the reason I asked both you and Frank here today is to let both of you know two things, first; since we entered in this consulting partnership an opportunity has presented itself to me that I can not in good conscious pass on. Additionally it will require extensive travel in the middle east. Now keeping in mind our developing relationship I wanted both of you to know that I will continue to be involved in our partnership however a great deal of the face to face contact will be between you Sharon and you Frank. I know Sharon for many years and I trust her instincts and business savvy so in the event you can not reach me in a timely manner I give her my full confidence and authority to obligate me. And secondly more directly to you Frank, I am hoping to be listed as one of your brother's personal advisors for travel and access purposes. What would something like that cost me?"

Frank sat back and said, "That is very expensive, very expensive. It would allow you to travel with full privileges of Michael's good name and that is not something he would take lightly."

Stephen said, "I understand, but a ballpark figure will do."

Frank said, "A bond will be required probably in the range of $10 million dollars, that alone would cost you $1 million and then his standard fee and of course my gratuity this could be rather expensive. Maybe you should consider an alternative, something less costly."

Stephen smiled and said, "What will it cost? I understand it is not something to take lightly even if the was not a consideration to either of us. Please."

Frank said, "With the bond, the fee and the gratuity around $5 million dollars. Now remember the bond is renewable every 12 months for an additional 10% or $100,000. As long as there are no problems you can travel under his privilege and receive access under his name as long as I approve it. If there is a problem you will be left to your own devices and we will not lift a finger to help you. Is that clear?"

Stephen responded, "Very clear. I will have the wired to you this evening."

Frank said, "Good, now I must run. Busy, busy, busy you know? ...Dr. Romani always a pleasure to see such a beautiful and intelligent woman. Good day."

And as he left, Stephen walked out to go to his office and wire the money to Frank's account.

Sharon waited in the study for about five minutes just long enough for Stephen to begin the wire transfer process but no complete it and then she walked over to his office. She stepped in and he said, "Oh! You still here? I'll be finished in a minute just penning a note to Frank."

Sharon stepped behind Stephen as he sat at his desk and said, "You're running aren't you?"

Stephen stopped writing and looked up at her and said, "No I have a business opportunity that is just to good to pass up on and it is going to take me out of the country for long periods of

U.S. Marshal Harry Bailey and the Case of the Deadly Psychologist

time but I didn't want either you or Frank to get the wrong impression, that's all."

Sharon stood back and began to walk towards the small table bar in the office. She spoke as she walked and said, "You coward. If you hadn't put all of that money with Frank the other week you would have left me holding the bag?"

Stephen pushed back from his desk and looked at her and said, "You can't be serious we have too much going on here to just up and walk away."

Sharon poured herself a vodka on the rocks then walked back over to the desk where Stephen was sitting. As she began her rant he stood up and the two were nose to nose when she said, "You little weasel you just bought a pass from Frank to travel between countries with and without extradition agreements with the U.S. and you think I didn't realize that? You are going to leave me holding the bag aren't you?"

Stephen looked down his glasses and into Sharon's eyes and said, "Preposterous, I would never do that to you. We have too much history together."

Then Sharon stepped back and as her purse fell to the floor she said, "You're lying" and she shot him twice in the chest.

When Stephen fell to the floor Sharon quickly emptied her glass on his clothes. Then she grabbed her purse and put the empty glass in it. Then she sat down at the desk and looked at what Stephen was doing. She realized he hadn't completed the wire transfer neither the instructions for the recipient so she wrote:

U.S. Marshal Harry Bailey and the Case of the Deadly Psychologist

'Frank I made one change in my plan, please add Dr. Romani as my associate with all the same rights a privileges. Let me know if there will be any additional charges and I will settle up asap. Thanks Stephen.' Then she executed the transfer.

She turned the laptop off and put it under her arm and quietly slipped out of the house. By the time she had drove off it was 6:45 p.m. so she used a throw away cell phone she had in her glove compartment and called the Sag Harbor Police Department and reported she had heard several gun shots coming from her neighbor's front yard as she was walking her dog.

U.S. Marshal Harry Bailey and the Case of the Deadly Psychologist

CHAPTER 5

LIFE ON THE RUN

6:45 p.m. Monday, September 4th 35 Clear View Drive, Sag Harbor, NY

It was just starting to get dark when I pulled up to the hidden circular six car driveway in front of Dr. Romani estate. The placed was beautifully landscaped hidden from the street but very open once inside the property line. I drove my car and Marshal Laura drove an unmarked SUV with an two man arrest team inside of it and they were followed by second two man arrest team in a marked car. Something didn't seem quite right when I pulled down the street and saw two police cars parked across from the residence on either side of the hidden driveway but I pulled inside anyway.

The plan was that once inside the property I would park and get out to approach the house and then less than a minute later Laura and the arrest teams would slowly pull in behind me. The point was for me to flush out the situation and then the shock and awe would rush in, little did I know what was about to happen.

What seemed to have happen shortly before I pulled in two

U.S. Marshal Harry Bailey and the Case of the Deadly Psychologist

local cops had responded to the scene for whatever reason and had begun a search of the properties perimeter before entering. I pulled in just as the two cops were coming from around the back of the property. I surprised them and they surprised me. The problem was I was a tall black man and they were to average white cops.

Both of them began to scream at me, telling me to get down on the ground. I tried to tell them that I was on the job and that they were about to blow my cover. After the third volley of screams Marshal Laura and the back up arrest team pulled into the driveway. At that point the two white cops were becoming even more confused and afraid. Especially when this beautiful Dominican woman stepped out of that Ford Explorer with a bullet proof vest on and a U.S. Marshal Badge hanging in front of it.

I raised my hands and said, "Look we are here to execute an arrest warrant of Dr. Romani and search the premises, please stand down."

Before the lead officer could say a word the butler came running out of the front door screaming that Mr. Hamilton had been shot and killed.

I said, "Where is Dr. Romani?"

The butler said, "Dr. Romani left earlier, I don't know exactly when though why?"

When he said why I just had to respond, so I said, "Do you know where she went?"

U.S. Marshal Harry Bailey and the Case of the Deadly Psychologist

He said, "No, why would I know that?"

I said, "What time are her guest supposed to arrive?"

He looked at me with a very strange look in his eyes and said, "What guest?"

Then both Laura, the lead officer and I stepped up closer to him and I said, "Dr. Romani invited me to a business gathering here for 7:30 p.m. Have any of the other guest arrived?"

Then the Butler said, "I'm sorry sir, but it seems as though you are operating under a misunderstanding, Dr. Romani is a business associate of the owner Mr. Hamilton and he is lying dead in his office. I'm sorry sir there are no plans for any kind of a business gathering at 7:30 p.m."

At that point I turned to the lead police officer and said, "This is what I need. One of you should call your dispatcher and ask them to send out a homicide team and explain to the dispatcher that a team of Marshal's is going to take over the scene until we figure out what happen to our fugitive. And by the way we have a witness warrant for the owner of this property as well. Now the other will come with us to witness and secure the scene until your guys get here and we can officially do this. Make it happen."

6:45 a.m. Tuesday, September 5th Marshal Regional Office

My supervisor Marshal Cooke walked into my office and said, "Harry! You had one job and only one job. When I got up this morning and turned on the news what do I see? 'Big headlines, in the midst of multi agency response to millionaires Sag Harbor estate, chaos and confusion delays U.S. Marshal's find of dead key witness. No suspects identified yet.' What happened?"

I said, "Boss it wasn't me, it was that arrest team you sent me with."That was when we both busted out laughing. After a minute or so Marshal Laura walked in and we all walked over to Marshal Cooke's office to review the evening's events.

I handed Marshal Cooke my investigation and incident reports and then summarized the events that took place. Then we talked about our next move. I said, "We know Hamilton was shot with a s&w .38 at close range. While there were no prints left behind by Dr. Romani we did find prints on a martini glass from a Frank Bloomberg the brother of former Mayor Bloomberg. So he is first on the list of witnesses. We know he comes into City Hall every day as if his brother is still in charge and goes and makes phone calls from his office between 9:00 a.m. and 10:30 a.m. as if he still works there, so we plan to visit him there this morning. Our best witness is the butler, he I.D. Dr. Romani's arrival but not her departure. That coupled with the lack of fingerprint evidence makes me think she killed Hamilton and tried to cover her tracks. We did note that a laptop, Hamilton's, is missing. We figure she took it to further cover up her being at the seen. Maybe we will get more out of Bloomberg on that when we talk to him. We sent an arrest team to Dr. Romani's office and apartment but so far no sign of her. Laura!"

Marshal Laura said, "I have checked the airports and there is no sign that she took a flight unless she used an alias we are still checking. Neither of her cars is missing so if she is traveling she

U.S. Marshal Harry Bailey and the Case of the Deadly Psychologist

has an unknown means of transportation."

Bert asked if we put out an APB on her and Laura said that she had. Then he said, "It's your mess go clean it up keep me informed." So we left his office and prepared to meet with Frank Bloomberg at City Hall.

Later that morning, 9:00 a.m., New York City, City Hall Frank Bloomberg's office

When Laura and I were escorted into Frank Bloomberg's office he did not seem to be surprised that we were there. He looked in to our eyes when he spoke he did not fidget when he spoke and he didn't seem nervous.

The first thing I said to him, was I guess you've seen the papers? And he said, "Of course, how can I help you?"

I said, "Tell us about the events that led up to yesterday's meeting at Stephen Hamilton's estate and then what happened while you were there."

Frank sat back in his desk chair and said, "We have a business relationship. The mayor is about to embark on a major redevelopment project, the likes which have never been seen anywhere in the world, right here in the Big Apple and Stephen and Sharon wanted to be a part of that. Stephen called for a meeting with Sharon and myself to let us know that he had planned to do a little traveling in the near future and wanted to assure us he was still committed to the project."

I said, "And what else?"

U.S. Marshal Harry Bailey and the Case of the Deadly Psychologist

Frank looked at Laura and me and said, "What do you mean, what else. That was it. There is nothing else I assure you."

I said, "You know I have been at this for many years and I have conducted many interviews and there is something else. So I suggest you tell us right here and right now because if I have to come back to you because I find that you have left something out I assure you I won't be in a forgiving mood."

Frank put his head down and then he thought for a moment and said, "Stephen wanted to be included on the mayors list of consultants so I accommodated him that is all."

I looked at Laura and let her know I was on to something, then I said, "Tell us more about being included on the mayor's list of consultants. Exactly what does that mean."

Frank started to get a little nervous and I said, "Look we are investigating a murder we are not the IRS but if you want us to give the regional director a call about this list of consultants and ask him what if any impact that activity has had or will have on the mayors and or your tax return this year, I will."

Frank sat up and said, "I certainly understand your position and I am trying to be as helpful as I can. Let me explain it this way, being included on the mayors list of consultants allows certain travel privileges and access privileges that most business people find of value. Simply put for a fee you can use the mayor's name to travel from any country to any country in the world. You can call any decision maker in the world and get an appointment. All we require is that they keep us informed of their activities."

U.S. Marshal Harry Bailey and the Case of the Deadly Psychologist

With that I said, "So what does it cost to get on the mayor's consultants list?"

Frank stuttered and then he said, "That I can not tell you."

Now I'm mad and I said, "You know you were doing fine. You were actually being helpful and non-obstructive to our investigation. So when I find out how much money is changing hands I will make that phone call to the IRS and the Treasury Department as well."

That was when I stood up and waited for Laura to stand as well.

Frank stood up and then he said, "The fee can range from a few thousand dollars to upwards of several million dollars. It is whatever the market will bare and the need for access that drives the number. This isn't personal its just business, you understand."

I turned to him one more time and said, "How much and give me an example of why it is so valuable."

Frank walked over to the office door and said, "Sometimes traveling from one country to another can be complicated and time consuming. Business people are under a lot of pressure when traveling and they like things to move smoothly. For example if I were to travel to certain places that have extradition treaties with the U.S. things would go smoothly. But if there were an occasion that I want to travel from a country with such an agreement to one that say did not have such an agreement there maybe unexpected delays, for whatever reason. Having access to the right people in one country or another might prove very valuable. Forward planning Marshal we offer them an opportunity to minimize delay's that is all."

I said, "Now I understand. Thank you for your cooperation." And we left.

2:00 p.m. Tuesday, September 5th Dr. Sharon Romani Office

Armed with a search warrant we secured all entrances and exits and then just kicked the front Lobby door open and proceeded up stairs to the office and then to the apartment of Dr. Sharon Romani. What were we looking for? Anything that might lead us to her whereabouts.

After about three hours we found little of nothing, no bank statements, no checks, no cre3dit card bills, no phone records, no journal's, no tax returns nothing it becoming more unbelievable then frustrating until on of the forensic team members knocked over a table lamp and an other stumbled on to a secret closet behind the good doctors office desk.

We searched the secret closet first and nothing was found in there of evidentiary value but it was interesting to know that she had the forethought to have the room built in the first place. What was of most interest was the cruel space we found behind the table lamp. There we found the mother load. Boxes of business records, bank statements, credit card statements and travel records.

It took five people two hours but we went through every document we pulled out of the cruel space and came up with the fact that our Dr. Romani had six separate business checking accounts at six different local bank branches. When Laura finished pulling all of that information together we found that the doctor still had varying amounts of cash in three of the accounts. Balances ranged from several thousand dollars to as much as several hundred thousand dollars in one. More importantly we realized one constant between to six bank branches; they all had safe deposit boxes available to account holders. So we split up the list and Laura and I each got three search warrants and took three branches each to visit.

6:00 p.m. Tuesday, September 5th Marshal's Regional Office

When we returned to the office after collecting the contents of the six safe deposit boxes it was no surprise to find that we had gathered a substantial hoard of cash and negotiable bonds. The final tally was $1.5 million in cash and over $3 million in bearer bonds and negotiable CD's.

Right then I knew she would be back or she would use whatever she could trust to retrieve the money and bonds. I don't think I got a chance to speak that thought to Laura because I remember as soon as it came to me, one of the crime scene investigators stepped in to my office and said, "We have confiscated everything of value from the doctor's office, apartment and home and secured it in our warehouse, but I thought you should know the Bentley will be going up for auction in 30 days."

It was light someone turned the light blub in my brain on full beam. I turned to Laura and said, "We need to hold onto that car. I know she will either come back for the cash, that is a given but I guaranty you she'll want to get that car back. That is a

RUTHLESS

beautiful machine and I know she took a lot of pride in it."

Laura smiled and said, "We have a special evidence warehouse in Newark I'll get a covered truck and send it there, we don't want anyone to know we still have it or where we have it. Maybe we'll have it collect a few tickets on its way over there as well. The notice in the mail might give them an incentive to retrieve it; I'll take care of it tonight."

8:00 p.m. Tuesday, September 5th, the Hotel Grand Cairo Lobby, Cape Town S.A.

Dr. Romani now traveling as Dr. Stephanie Hamilton walked up to the Hotel registration desk and asked for a room for a room. When the Desk Clerk asked her how long she planned to stay she said, "I'm going to be taking a few overnight and weekend junkets over the next several weeks but most of my business will be here in Cape Town can you accommodate me for 30 days?"

The Desk Clerk said, "Of course we can however Madame if you would prefer a chalet over looking the mountains and the city we can book you at our Whitehead Facility the accommodations are five star as well but the price is much more affordable?"

Stephanie smiled and said, "What is the cost here?"

The Desk Clerk responded, "$5,000 U.S. per day. The cost of the chalet which is about twice the size as our King suite here is just over $3,500 U.S. per day."

Then Stephanie said, "Can I book a chalet but have my

U.S. Marshal Harry Bailey and the Case of the Deadly Psychologist

messages, and mail forwarded from here, there?"

The Desk Clerk responded, "Of course not a problem many of our regular guest request that all of the time. If you will just step into our business center and set up an account while I make the arrangements for your chalet you will find that everything you need to be in two places at the same time can be set up there. It is as easy as 1, 2, 3 click."

Then Stephanie said, "If anyone comes looking for me, I'll be notified of their interest?"

The Desk Clerk responded, "Not a problem as you wish."

Later that evening at the White Head Mountain Resort

No sooner did Stephanie arrive, toured her suite and unpack her overnight bag while she was pouring herself a drink there was a knock at her door. When she opened it, it was her brother Donald. She hugged him and kissed him on the cheek and he walked in and took a seat out on the veranda.

The view of the city of Cape town was breathtaking and the warm late summer night was calm and quiet. When Stephanie walked out to join Donald she brought him a drink as well and the two just sat across from each other for a little while just looking and enjoying the view.

After a short time Donald spoke and said, "Sis the state came in like gang busters and shut everything down, the accounts, the credit cards the cell phones. It's all over for the business. I got out of there by the skin of my teeth."

RUTHLESS

Stephanie smiled and said, "Good job. How much cash did you get out of the accounts and safe deposit boxes?"

Donald said, "Not much. Stephen had run through most of it. I barely got half a mil. That's not going to last very long at these hotel rates, you know? And besides Cindy is due any day now and I got to get back for the babies birth."

Stephanie said, "Don't worry about it, we'll be out of here is a week. We'll buy a house on the water, a duplex, and then next week you'll go back and clear out my safe deposit boxes and we will be good until we do something else. Maybe open a bar on the beach or buy one. The only problem is my car. My baby. I'm gonna need you to ship it back here."

Donald responded and said, "Sharon you are not listening to me. I'm out. I can't be running off and ducking and dodging the police the rest of my life. I want to settle down, marry and raise a family and Cindy wants that as well. Besides that car of yours is going to be the death of you. Why don't you just sell it and take the money and buy another one, for God sake?"

Stephanie smiled and said, "Why don't I just turn you in to the cops and go find a new brother?"

Donald said, "You make light of this situation. I'm not going to jail for you or your stupid car."

Then Stephanie said, "Look the car is at the house by the time the state finishes taking Stephen's offices and books apart you'll be back from vacation, slip into town, visit your sister's place and take the car for a spin, right to the docks. Pay my broker his

RUTHLESS

fee, get the insurance and Walla before you know I'll be picking it up in Cape town."

9:00 a.m. Wednesday, September 13th Marshal's Regional Office

Laura and I had been notified that the State Finance Commissioner's Office had finally completed its forensic audit Of Stephen Hamilton's brokerage operation and planned to stop by this morning to update us and the DA.

ADA April Montgomery was assigned to the case. This was her first murder case although economic crimes were her specialty. How she managed to draw this case I don't know. Maybe it was the luck of the draw but after being in the DA's office for almost 10 years and rising to the position of Bureau Chief she had probably seen ever trick in the book so a murder case was way overdue.

ADA Montgomery was a soft spoken plus size African American female with a strong background in litigation so I knew we were in good hands.

When State Controllers Audit Chief Angelo Garcia stepped into the conference room everyone was prepared to be overwhelmed and confused before whatever he had to say would settle in, but surprisingly he wasn't long winded and he was rather clover.

He told us that Hamilton's house of cards had been on the rocks for sometime and his death merely put him out of his own misery. While his firm managed thousands of clients he only

U.S. Marshal Harry Bailey and the Case of the Deadly Psychologist

had one stockbroker working full time. He had a boiler room of about 50 unlicensed brokers making calls and soliciting business. Usually what happened when they signed up a new client they got a nice commission and went right back to calling on new business. Those that finished getting their licenses were pretty much run off to start a new career with a more reputable brokerage firm but discouraged from taking any of the clients they earned with him based on a no compete contract they all signed when they joined his firm.

He went on to tell us that the only way he continued in business was his only broker would file a false agency insurance certificate with the state department. Typically what he did was find an small and hungry insurance firm give them the name of a shell brokerage firm as the insured and them alter the binding certificate and submit it by hand at the very last minute. The file clerk merely update the computer system at the state level and they bought yet another year to operate.

He said as far as books and records what ever the firm sent to the state or to customers was really just made up statements and accounting reports. Not one thread of truth in any of them except the date at the top of the page. Typically what they would do is open an account with a deposit and an automatic deposit agreement. Then he would pay whatever bills needed to be paid, sometimes he would send dividend checks to selected clients and he would pocket the rest.

He gave us a typical case, the accounts both Laura and I opened several weeks earlier.

He told us that within two weeks Hamilton had drained our

deposits and spent them planning to use our monthly payments to pay any dividends that might be made up from the fictitious investments he planned for our portfolios. Additionally he said, Hamilton was requiring and or falsifying credit insurance on all of his clients using his name as the sole beneficiary. So if you would have made a claim against him all he had to do was wait until things calmed down and then file for reimbursement of any lose he suffered. Finally we noted that on several accounts Hamilton was named executor of the client's estate. Now under the right circumstances he could sale all of the client's assets at one price and hand over a lesser amount to the beneficiaries while covering certain losses in the stock portfolio along with his fees. He concluded saying Hamilton was a master theft, his financial situation at death was his mansion was in foreclosure, his household staff salaries were two weeks overdue, his cars were about to be reprocessed, all of his high end watches and jewelry were on loan or under pawn, he did have $1,000,000 in cash in a wall safe and another $3,000,000 spread out in 10 different safe deposit boxes. His vacation homes were under leases that were about to lapse.

Then he said, "If you asked where all the money went I would have to say gone for a lavish life style but there was one no two things that I thought would be of interest to your office in particular."

I said, "Please tell us."

He said, "From all accounts over the twenty year life of his brokerage firm two people seemed to receive the greatest financial benefit. His second in command at the firm a Donald

U.S. Marshal Harry Bailey and the Case of the Deadly Psychologist

Romani and his psychologist a Dr. Sharon Romani; between the two we can account for close to $5,000,000 in addition to commissions and salary going to Donald and another $3,000,000 in commissions and other miscellaneous payments going to Dr. Romani. Now although Hamilton's record keeping was not maintained according to generally accepted accounting principals he did keep a personal journal with copious notes."

Needless to say before the auditor left Marshal Laura put out an APB for Donald Romani.

10:00 p.m. Thursday, September 14th JFK International Airport South African Airways Terminal 6

Donald Romani hurried through the airport terminal to the fly and drive car rental lot where a blue and black interior Lincoln continental was gassed up and waiting. He through his luggage in the trunk and took off like a bat out of hell. He had several stops to make before having to take a long drive to connect with his return flight at Newark International Airport at 9:00 p.m. later that evening and he had to go by the hospital to see Cindy and the baby first.

11:00 a.m. Mercy Hospital Midtown Manhattan-Paternity Ward

Donald hurried into the maturity ward were the Head Nurse told him everything was fine he was now the proud father of a beautiful baby girl named Melissa and his fiancé was resting in room 312. Donald went down stairs to the hospital lobby and picked up the biggest bouquet of flowers they had and went directly to see Cindy.

When Donald entered Cindy's room she perked up and started to cry tears of joy. She told him all about the birth and had the nurse bring the birth certificate so he could sign it and make Melissa Romani officially his daughter. After the signing of the birth certificate Donald tried to explain to Cindy that he was only in town for the day but he would be back for good in a week. Cindy begged him not to go but in the end she understood he had to finish helping his sister in her time of need. Cindy reluctantly agreed to let him go but before he left she asked him if he would change his life insurance policies to reflect both her and little Melissa just in case something went horribly wrong while he was travelling across the ocean and he agreed.

First Stop 12:00 noon

At 12:00 noon Donald arrived at 603 3rd Avenue in New York, Bank Leumi of New York its 3rd Ave. Branch office. Donald pulled up to the pay for parking lot across from the bank branch and told the parking clerk he would be less than 30 minutes. He walked around the corner past the bank branch office to the FedEx Kiosk and bought a large mailbag. Then he walked back around the corner and went into the bank branch where he proceeded to the safe deposit clerk's desk. Once there he requested access to his sister's box where he was also a signatory. Since he had the right to access the box if his sister was with him or if he had both keys, which he did.

Inside the safe deposit box vault he empty close to $300,000 in brand new shrink wrapped dollar bills from the extra large safe deposit box into his Fed Ex bag and then returned to the FedEx kiosk around the corner to repackage the money in a very large television box and then posted it back to Cape town.

Second Stop 12:00 noon

At 1:00 pm Donald made his way downtown to the 2nd Ave. U-Haul Storage facility where he parked in the storage lot and accessed a 4' x 4 x 10' unit in his sister's name. This time he merely grabbed two suitcases which contained close to $500,000, again, in brand new shrink wrapped dollar bills. He immediately took the suitcases to the nearest FedEx Kiosk boxed up the suitcases and posted them back to Sharon in Cape Town.

Third Stop 2:30 p.m.

This time Donald had to drive clear across Manhattan to post another large package to his sister Sharon. He drove over to 12th Ave. and 54th Street to another Self Storage facility where he picked up four smaller suitcases containing another $500,000 and quickly went to the nearest UPS MailBox Center and again posted them directly Sharon.

That was when he stopped for lunch near the Javits Center just before he drove through the tunnel towards Newark International Airport and its cargo hangars and warehouses.

When he got to Warehouse 27B the Federal Law Enforcement Auto Auction Center he pulled up to the security guard gate and announced himself as Frederick Murphy of Auto World Inventory Associates and showed his I.D. and drove into the lot.

U.S. Marshal Harry Bailey and the Case of the Deadly Psychologist

Inside the lot he parked and milled around with the over one hundred other prospective buyers until the auction began at 4:00 p.m.

The first car to go up for auction was Sharon's Bentley. It had over $5,000 in parking and towing tickets and fees on it and the bidding started at $5,500. The first bid came for the far end of the crowd and it was from a woman who bid $75,000. The second bid came from a tall black man standing behind him for $100,000. Before Donald could get his hand up and his mouth open to bid the auctioneer had accepted a bid for $245,000. Finally Donald said, $300,000 and the place went quiet for about 20 seconds, just long enough for everyone in the place to get a good look at him then it was pure pandemonium.

The crowd closed in on him and all he could feel was the weight of four 200 plus pound men holding him down on the floor. All he could say was wait a minute I only have a check and its not even signed. Then I said, "Don't worry we take MasterCard or Visa." He looked at me as if he had lost his mind and then I said, "Let him up. Donald Romani you are under arrest for aiding and abiding a fugitive from justice. I am now going to read you your rights..."

9:00 p.m. Later that evening –Marshal Regional Office Interrogation Room B

Donald Romani sat waiting for his attorney to show up with a smug look on his face so I asked him what was up with the smug look on his face and he said, "I don't know why you people are waiting my time with these trumped up charges that will never stick. When my attorney finishes with you, you will both be

U.S. Marshal Harry Bailey and the Case of the Deadly Psychologist

lucky to have jobs as meter maids."

I looked back at him and said, "My arrest and conviction record is 99.9% to .01% do you know what that means? Let me tell you what that means. It means there is one tenth of a percentage point between going home free tonight and me having you convicted of tampering with evidence in a multiple murder and securities fraud case."

He said, "What proof do you have that I tampered with any evidence?"

That was when both his attorney and Marshal Allen walked in. His attorney belted out that the interview was over and he wanted time to speak with his client. Marshal Allen stepped in and said, "Harry we found something you need to see." And he handed me a folder with some papers in it, so Marshal Laura and I got up and walked out into the hallway to check it out.

When we finally stepped back into the interview room Donald's attorney confidently said, "What proof do you have that my client has tampered with any evidence in your murder fraud case?"

That was when I laid it on him, I dropped the folder marshal Allen had handed me earlier on the table and said, "Let's start from the top. Where have you been the last week?"

He said, "What has that got to do with anything?"

I said, "I, we already know. What were you doing at the auto auction in Newark?"

U.S. Marshal Harry Bailey and the Case of the Deadly Psychologist

He looked at his attorney and his attorney said, "What relevance does that have?"

I said, "I already know."

Then I said, "What do you think your sister is going to do when the packages that you sent her don't arrive?"

He turned beet red and his attorney looked at him and said, "Hold on a minute." Then the two began to whisper to each other. After a couple of minutes the attorney said, "What's on the table?"

I said, "You looking for a deal? What do you have to offer?"

His attorney nodded for Donald to go ahead and speak freely.

Donald spoke and said, "One of those packages is mine. It is money I earned I just included it in one of the packages I sent her for convenience. You will keep that in mind?"

I started laughing and said, "My friend any funds gained or earned as you call it from an illegal and fraudulent venture either before or after the act is subject to forfeiture. You aren't going to get a dime of that money. What you need to do is start focusing on getting your sentence down to something before retirement age. What, how old are you 35? You managed all of the firm's clients some 2 or 3 thousand accounts? At 18 months per your looking at 18 to 54 thousand months! That would be slightly passed retirement I would say; right Marshal Laura?"

Donald jumped up and started to shout, he said, "I earned that money legitimately through commissions earned and I and my

U.S. Marshal Harry Bailey and the Case of the Deadly Psychologist

family are entitled to every dime of it. Any extra money I got from Stephen was because he wanted to make sure I kept quiet. I never asked for a dime of it. If he gave me a Christmas bonus or a vacation bonus that was it and that was earned. I worked hard for him and anything illegal was on him not me." Then he just hung his head and said, "So what can you do for me?"

I smiled and said, "Tell us the truth, nothing but the truth and we will gladly tell the DA that you have cooperated fully and we will ask her to work with you on that money issue. Lie to us and all bets are off. Is that clear?"

Donald's attorney nodded again and Donald said; he was just a messenger and an errand boy for the last 10 years. He said he was recruited right out of college to work in Hamilton's boiler room operation and he just never left, even after he figured out what Hamilton was doing. He told us Sharon had sent him back to retrieve her cash and car. And that they had planned to buy a couple of beach bungalow and a tiki bar on the beach of Cape Town and relax for a while.

He made it clear that he had nothing to do with any of the murders and that h only found out about them in passing or in the newspaper. He told us that Sharon was staying at the Grand Hotel in Cape Town one of their chalets over looking the city and mountains. And he gave us her address art the hotel. Before he was booked and arraigned Laura and I left to take jump seats on an Air Force C-130 out of McGuire Air Force Base in New Jersey.

It took more time flying to get there than I ever imagined but by the time we landed and checked in with the local Police I knew we were just too late.

10:00 a.m. Sunday, September 17th Cape Town International Airport Runway 3L Military Access Only

Luckily we were able to clear customs as we coordinated arrival and intent with local authorities. By the time we arrived at the Cape Town Grand Hotel it was noon and a full day later than the boxes Donald would have shipped to Sharon had we not intercepted them, would have arrived. Our game plan was to arrest her as she retrieved the boxes but she never showed up. We waited until 4:00 pm the last pick up time and no Sharon. We figured since the boxes did not arrive the day before she just didn't buy the store that both he and the boxes where unavoidable late. We went to her suite and found that she had not been there for almost two days. Then we went to the night desk clerk who told us that he had seen her leave earlier that weekend but he wasn't sure when. When we pressed for more information he said he remembered she asked about overland travel accommodations to Namibia. He said she mentioned doing of sight seeing on the river there. That was the one thing we didn't want to happen, her moving into a country were we had no extradition agreements in place. Laura asked if she turned in her key and the clerk said, no she hadn't. That was when I called the boss to let him know what we were facing and he in no uncertain terms instructed us to return on the next thing smoking, flying, rolling or sliding. He said we took a chance and lost so cut our losses and get back asap besides he said he had some news for us. When I pressed him for details he just said, "I'll tell you when I see you and hung up.

CHAPTER 6

DO NOT PASS GO

**8:00 p.m. Sunday, September 17th JFK International Airport
South African Airways Terminal**

Dr. Romani wasted no time leaving Cape Town late Friday night when the packages of cash she had expected did not show up at her chalet. Dressed down in jeans and sneakers she made her way to the terminal transportation gate and took a cab to Donald's apartment and arrived just minutes after he returned from having dinner with his attorney.

Sharon had a key to Donald's apartment so she let herself in and made herself comfortable. When Donald arrived from the police station and opened the door to his two bedroom duplex on the upper Westside of Central Park all of the lights were out as expected. He made his way into the kitchen area and cut on a foyer light on his way there.

Even though he had just eaten he immediately looked in the refrigerator and as he bent down to look in the freezer compartment he was struck hard on the back of his head. The blow had so much force behind it, it knocked him out cold.

When he woke up he found himself tied to a chair with duck

U.S. Marshal Harry Bailey and the Case of the Deadly Psychologist

tape with a dish rag stuffed in his mouth. He looked around and noticed a bucket of water sitting on the floor in front of him and then he focused on Sharon sitting on the sofa across the room smoking a cigarette and sipping on a martini.

He tried to ask her to untie him and she just sat there as if not to hear a word he screamed through the towel in his mouth.

After several attempts to get her to untie him he realized what was about to happen and he used every ounce of his strength to wiggle, shake, bounce and rock his way loose to no avail.

Finally Sharon finished her drink and her cigarette and got up and slowly walked over to the chair Donald was sitting in. She pulled the towel in his mouth out just far enough to hear what he was saying. When he finished begging for his life and telling her how much he wanted to call her to let her know what was going on but his attorney held him up.

Sharon smiled and said, "I understand Donald. That's just not the problem. The real problem is the cops have my money. Now I remember telling you don't keep any receipts. I said remember Donald after each post take the receipt and mail it to me, overnight right then and there, wherever you posted the cash from. But good old Donald, you just couldn't follow the simplest directions could you? That was the only way those fools could have possibly intercepted the money after they caught you. And where did they catch you at? The auction right? I knew it. So anyway what did they promise you for giving me up? A lighter sentence? A new car perhaps? Or a free ticket back to Cape Town? You really don't have to answer those questions I already know the answers. Now, now, now what do we do with you

U.S. Marshal Harry Bailey and the Case of the Deadly Psychologist

now?"

Sharon continued to talk as she lifted up the bucket of water and began to pour it on the towel in Donald's mouth. He fought so hard to keep the water from soaking through the towel he tipped over backwards which just made it easier for Sharon to continue to slowly pour the water down his throat.

Once the bucket was empty Donald stopped squiring and just laid very still and quietly.

That was when she finished searching his apartment and his body for his safe deposit key, which she found in the cleverly modified watchband he was wearing on his wrist.

8:00 a.m. Monday, September 18th Marshal Regional Office Supervising Marshal Cooke's Office

Marshal Laura and I had barely taken a seat in front of Marshal Cooke's desk when he said, "You two relaxed from your globetrotting? You know while you were sunning it in beautiful Cape Town your suspect was here gutting your case?"

I couldn't believe it and neither could Laura and then he dropped the bombshell, he said, "Donald, your star witness is dead. His downstairs neighbor called the super about a water leak in his apartment and when he found the body in the middle of the living room floor he called NYPD who called us. We shut down any possible flights out for her or anybody who even looks like her so I believe she is still in town. Now it is your turn to start doing your job and bring this killing machine in. Let me know whatever you need but we got 48 hours before I have to call in the troops."

I said, "The FBI?"

And he said, "You know how this works. This has gotten out of hand. I got more calls on this than I can count. Hell even I'm holding by a thread. Keep me in the loop on a hour by hour contact. Now go."

Laura and I went back to my office to think through this mess and see what to do next. We agreed that there are no more witnesses worth eliminating and if so if Sharon had already made it out of the country to a place where we could not take hold of her why would she risk capture to return and kill her own brother; was the question. When we looked at it that way we realized that there had to be a strong motive for her to make the trip all the way back to New York and the only reason that made since was money. I thought we had confiscated all the money the she had but Laura seemed to believe that Donald must have had some stashed away that we didn't know about but Sharon did.

With that we figured, if it works why change it, there must be a safe deposit box out there with Donald Romani name on it the question is where could it be. I remembered him saying that one of the boxes we confiscated was actually his, he just sent his money in her box so many be she realized he would have held something back just in case. And that lead me to think that maybe he had a personal safe deposit box at one of the banks he visited while collecting her cash. So we decided to back track each of the overnight stations he used to post the boxes of cash to the most likely bank with a safe deposit service in the vicinity

U.S. Marshal Harry Bailey and the Case of the Deadly Psychologist

and see if he had a personal box.

We knew it was a long shot but it made sense and time was no longer on our side, because if that was the reason Sharon returned and killed Donald then she already knows where the money is.

9:00 a.m.

We stopped in at the 603 3rd Avenue Branch of the Bank Leumi of New York 3rd Ave. Branch office at 9:00 a.m. just as they were opening up for the day. We spoke to the Branch Manager and the Safe Deposit box clerk and while Donald had been in there late last week he did not own a box personally. That took us 20 minutes to find out.

10:00 a.m. the second stop

At 10:00 a.m. Laura and I were parked in front of the 2nd Ave. U-Haul Storage facility surveying the area for a bank with safe deposit box services when Laura spotted Dr. Romani going into the lobby. And from the looks of it the good doctor recognized Laura as well. By the time we jumped out of the car and ran across the street Sharon was no where in sight. So we split up, Laura searched each floor of the storage unit and I talk with the Clerk to see if they recognized a picture of Donald and attempted to find out if he had a unit in the facility.

When I finished with the Clerk I had found out that Donald have a small unit, and it was right next to his now empty sisters unit. I caught up with Marshal Laura who had searched all 8 floors looking for Sharon, and we had the Clerk open Donald's unit.

U.S. Marshal Harry Bailey and the Case of the Deadly Psychologist

Inside we found close to $250,000 in cash and another $2,000,000 in bearer bonds and CD's. It took us almost 3 hours to complete the process of finding the money, getting the search warrant hand delivered, securing the evidence and returning to the office to begin the paperwork.

By the time we finished that I just assumed Dr. Romani was back in her hide out making plans to find some other hidden stash, so I left the office around 4:00 p.m. and went home to get some long needed sleep.

12:00 noon Joe Reese's apartment (Marshal Bailey's neighbor)

Dressed in a dark blue suite with a white silk blouse Sharon pulled in front of Joe Reese's apartment building and waited for the door man to come out and ask her to move. She kept looking from the drivers side through the passenger side window at the door man and then writing something on a clipboard she had resting on the steering wheel.

Finally the Door man left his post in the building lobby and walked out to her car and said, "You are parked in a no waiting zone, can I help you?"

Dr. Romani said, "Yes I am from State Farm Insurance and I have an appointment to do an estimate on a tenants apartment, there was a gas explosion a few days ago, in."

The Door man laughed and said, "Lady that was over a month ago, boy you people must be really backed up?"

Then Dr. Romani said, "Look can I leave my car here and run in?

RUTHLESS

U.S. Marshal Harry Bailey and the Case of the Deadly Psychologist

I have six other stops to make before I get off."

The Door man said, "Look Lady if I let you stand here one more minute I'm gonna loss my job why don't you pull around to the residents underground parking garage and I'll just buzz you in from there. You know what apartment it is right?"

Dr. Romani said, "Thank you and yes I have him in apartment 6B."

Sharon pulled into the resident's underground garage and the Door men buzzed her into the building giving her access to the elevator bank. When Sharon got up to Joe's apartment she knocked on the door. Joe wasn't expecting anyone, since the Door man usually buzzes in visitors so Joe assumed it was one of the neighbors and he just opened the front door and Sharon tased him immediately. When he woke up he was duck taped to a chair in his living room while Sharon was quietly but methodically dismantling the temporary wall put up between Joe's and Marshal Bailey's apartment after his son Mark's attempted assassination.

When Joe started to scream for help Sharon walked back over and to him and duck taped his mouth closed. Then she returned to opening the partially rebuilt wall in the pantry where Mark's gas leak had did the most damage.

After a short period of time she was able to open a large enough opening where she could access my apartment and then she did.

She literally cruelled through the opening she had made into my

U.S. Marshal Harry Bailey and the Case of the Deadly Psychologist

apartment and set up a trap for me.

4:30 p.m. Marshal Bailey's apartment

At around 4:15 or 4:30 p.m. I unlocked my apartment door and stepped inside of my foyer. As usual I take my weapon, unload it and place it and the holster in the drawer of my French writing desk I have in my foyer along with my badge and I.D. No sooner did I complete those two task do I find myself literally shaking and quaking in my loafers; she tased me.

When I woke up I was double duck taped to a kitchen chair sitting in the middle of my living room looking at Sharon seated on my sofa drinking a martini and smoking a cigarette.

With a little tough in cheek I said, "Ok Sharon you can untie me. We've had enough fun." It wasn't much of a surprise to see her slowly get up, take a sip of her drink, put her smoke down and slowly walk over and slap the hell out of me. But what was surprising was the fact that I didn't realize she was as strong as she was. I almost passed out. When I pulled myself together I said, "Have you lost your ever loving mind. Kidnapping a federal marshal is a bigger offense then the murders your already charged with if that is even possible." She hauled off and slapped me again. That was when I got mad and really tried to pull away from the chair but that duck tape was a lot stronger than I thought.

Then there was a thump next door and she quickly walked away. I could see where she had broke through the pantry wall from Joe Reese's apartment and she went right back through

RUTHLESS

that opening.

After about a minute she came back and stood in front of me. By now I figured she was in charge until things turned in my favor so I kept my mouth shut this time.

Finally she spoke and said, "Where is my money?"

I just looked at her. She spoke and repeated herself and I continued to look her dead in the eye. I guess it was the third time she repeated the statement when she just hauled off and slapped me again this time knocking me so hard the chair I was sitting in fell over on its back as I slipped in and out of conscience.

It was around 6:30 p.m. when she poured a bucket of ice water across my face and woke me up. This time she was standing over me with a kitchen towel in one hand and the bucket of ice water in the other. I knew what that meant. I had to take this woman very seriously she had nothing to lose and she was desperate.

I hurriedly spoke and said, "Look your money is in evidence and there is no way they are going to give it to you for me and or Joe. The service is serious about not paying ransoms. Now if you untie me now I will tell them you came to your senses and realized the error you had made. I will tell them that you showed remorse and began to cooperate fully. Now how is Joe?"

She just looked at me and then she said, "I killed my only brother. I killed my best friend and I tried to kill you and blame it on your best friend and partner. All of the money I made is gone and my Bentley. Do you really think I give a damn about you and your silly line about surrendering or how much jail time I save? Really? Now if you don't come up with a valid solution in the next two minutes I am gonna make good on my attempt to kill you and your neighbor. Then I'll just walk out that door and leave you both here to rot. Tick tock, tick tock."

I had to think fast so I said, "If I gave you what the front money they gave me to reel Stephen in would that help you?"

She perked up and said, "How much is that?"

I said, "There is about $250,000 left. In a safe deposit box not far from here."

She said, "Where?"

I said, "What I maybe tied up but I ain't stupid. Let's cut this deal and make it real first."

She grabbed the towel and forced it in my mouth and started to pour some water on it. I wiggled and shook but it was of little help. Finally she stopped and pulled the towel out just far enough for me to speak and I said, "I believe you but I don't trust you. Now we can work together and both get what we want but you are going to have to trust me on this."

She put the bucket down and sat down on my chest and said, "Talk."

I said, "I have to call Marshal Laura, she has the second key to the safe deposit box. You got Joe over there, right? Is he still

RUTHLESS

alive? Hold on to him. Or better yet when Laura comes, you and her can go and get it, I'll wait here with Joe. That way you can go your way and she can return here and get us."

She said, "Explain."

I said, "Look the way it works is Marshal Laura has a key to a safe deposit box that has my key in it. Only she knows the number of the box and the location. I have a key to a safe deposit box with her key in it. Only I know the location of it. Then when we both have our second key we have to use them together to open the box where the money is, at a totally separate location. So neither of us can do anything without the other, you see? And neither of us can do anything during now business hours another fail safe."

She said, "I don't believe you."

I said, "Get her on the phone what do you have to loose?"

She thought about it for a minute and then she said, "Let me think about this. You hungry? Like a glass of water for dinner?"

I laid there on the living room floor for hours, she wouldn't even let me go to the bathroom, the place was a mess. Finally at about 3:00 a.m. she woke me up and as I laid on the floor taped to a kitchen chair and handed me my cellphone and said, "Call your Marshal Laura and tell her to get your key in the morning and bring it here, and don't say another word; here." And she put the phone to my ear as it rang.

Marshal Laura did not answer her cellphone so Sharon told me to leave a message, which was exactly what she wanted to

U.S. Marshal Harry Bailey and the Case of the Deadly Psychologist

happen.

6:00 a.m. the next morning

The next morning was when I found out what kind of a neat freak Dr. Romani was, when I woke up she had removed the duck tape and replaced it with my own handcuffs. She had rolled me over next to the sofa and cleaned up the spot I was laying in as well as changed my clothes and me too. I was a little stiff from laying on my right side for three hours but none the worst.

I guess it was 6:00 a.m. when she kicked me in the side and woke me up. She said, it was time to prepare for Marshal Laura's arrival. Her plan was have both Joe and me duck taped together, each on either side of the hole in the pantry wall and leave the gas leaking ever so slowly that neither of us cloaks to death. But if either of us makes a wrong move we would spark the gas and blow each other up, while Laura and her go and pick up the money.

I could see this woman was not only smart but resourceful the way she had figured out how to jerry rig Joe and I back to back with this ignition device between us was brilliant to say the least. She sat her cellphone on the floor in front of me, just out of my reach. Then she programmed it to strike a flame when she called it. But the one thing she over looked was the fact that both Joe and I were not only army veterans both battle tested and getting out of tight situations was in now apart of our DNA.

9:45 a.m. that morning

RUTHLESS

U.S. Marshal Harry Bailey and the Case of the Deadly Psychologist

Not having a clue that anything was wrong Marshal Laura went to the bank and retrieved my safe deposit box key and brought it to my apartment. When she rang the door bell Sharon opened the door as if it was me just standing behind the door, and Laura walked in and just like me Sharon tased her from behind.

Laura fell like a ton of bricks and Sharon quickly handcuffed her with her own handcuffs. When Laura woke up seated next to me she said, "You could have told me what to expect, Harry."

That was when I knew Laura had something up her sleeve.

Sharon walked over to Laura and said, "No talking, just listen. This is how this is going to go down. I am going to unhandcuff you and the both of us are going to go down and get the second safe deposit key and then we are going to go and get the cash from the third deposit box. When I get the money you will be free to return here and release your partner and his hostage on the other side of that pantry wall there. Now the quicker and efficiently we get through this the better chance your partner and his hostage will have at surviving this ordeal. Is that clear?"

Laura was very cooperative, even when Sharon took her handguns, maybe a little to cooperative for Sharon's taste but still cooperative. The two went to the bank and got the second safe deposit box key and then they went to the final bank to open the third box to get the cash. Once they were left alone in the close quarters safe deposit room, of the third bank which was probably a 4'x4' room to open the box Marshal Laura made her move.

Laura, an experienced street fighter is skillful in close quarters

RUTHLESS

she was able to strike Sharon quickly and effectively almost knocking her unconscious with the first two blows. But Sharon persevered and held her own, retaliating using the cash box as a ram and locked Laura's right arm against the closed door and head butting her. Laura went into kick boxing mode and delivered a right and left knee into Sharon's midsection forcing her to back up enough so Laura could regain use of her right arm. The ruckus caused the Safe Deposit Clerk and the Branch Manager to come to the booth the two women were in to see what was going on. When they opened the door it was just enough of a distraction for Sharon to use the chair in the room to again pin Marshal Laura against the far wall and pull her gun from the back of her waist band. She forced the Bank Manager and the Clerk inside at gunpoint. Took the safe deposit box and the chair out of the booth.

Once outside of the booth Sharon wedged the chair under the door handle, grabbed a money bag from the Safe Deposit Box Clerks desk drawer, put the cash in it and left the bank. It took Laura and the two bankers a few minutes to bust through the booth door and when they got out Laura called for back up to meet her at my place to make sure Joe and I survived.

U.S. Marshal Harry Bailey and the Case of the Deadly Psychologist

CHAPTER 7

Mad Money Or Bad Money

3:45 p.m. Wednesday, September 20th New York Thruway Exit 6

Sharon had made it almost to Niagara Falls with the cash in hand driving her brother's spare car, which we did not know about from searching his apartment; a mistake we took a lot of heat on. There was no way for us to know that she had made it that far we didn't know which way she had planned to travel or by what means she would use. As a matter of police procedure we put out an APB once Joe Reese and I were rescued but by then she had already had a 45 minute head start. Oh! And there was one other obstacle that prevented us from catching her before she made it that far was the fact that she had a blow up doll in the passenger seat of her car. As long as she stayed out of the HOV lanes there was no reason for an officer to consider stopping her because the alert indicated a single white female traveling alone.

The only way we found out that she had gotten that far was at that time was several days after she had fled the city and we lost track of her, she used one of the counterfeit bills in the stash of cash Laura had given her. Counterfeits are more effective because the likelihood of there being recognized and our receiving notification of same is greater then having to locate bills that have been marked.

She must have picked up a hike hiker at the Canadian border because again no vehicles were spotted being driven by single white females in the first 48 hours of her escape. And the counterfeit only told us that she wasn't aware she had counterfeits and that she was physically there at the border when it was passed. With that information we figured that she was going to take a scenic trip through Canada. Whether she was going to take up residence there or go to Europe or back to South Africa was a toss up. It depended on where her ultimate destination was.

But it wasn't long before she tipped her hand and at least we had her direction. About a week later some more of the counterfeit bills started to show up near the U.S. border between Oregon and Canada we figured she was either going to go north to Alaska or try to cross the water into Russia. Or worse case double back along the west coast towards Mexico.

What we later found out was shortly after she slipped out of the bank where she left Marshal Laura and the two bankers in the safe deposit booth, she stopped at a near by Fed Ex store and sent a bulk of the counterfeit cash to her hotel in Cape Town. We knew that because of the tracking device that was planted in the middle bungle of the cash. As long as the tracking device was stationary we knew she hadn't picked it up yet. So our plan was as soon as the money moved we would move.

Counterfeit bills continued to show up in small amounts from

U.S. Marshal Harry Bailey and the Case of the Deadly Psychologist

various locations letting us know that she had not left Canada but she was still on the move, when finally she gave us our first big break and bought and charted a private plane to take her from Edmonston Canada back to Cape Town. When the FBO agent monitoring the Counterfeit bills found out who had deposited them into a local Canadian bank he flew up and meet with the man.

The Agent reported his interview to our office that same day. He told us the man a Canadian citizen who worked as a private pilot for hire for a number of high profile business executives and entertainer, said Sharon was referred to him by a good client so he took the clients word even before he meet her. He said she asked him if he would take her to France for two days and then to Cairo and then to Cape Town. He said that would be a rather long trip and she would be expected to pay for his accommodations as well as all landing and turnaround fees. He said he quoted her a price of $50,000 U.S. and she agreed. He told her he would be available with 24 hours notice and she agreed to that.

Of course when we heard that we were ready to go pick her up right then but the agent said, unfortunately as he was interviewing the pilot Sharon showed up and demanded they leave right then. The Agent said, "He could not arrest her because he did not have an arrest warrant for her that would allow him to take her out of the country on a murder charge. The passing of counterfeit bills would have had to be processed in Canada and then extradition proceedings would have had to be initiated and that could take months. So he decided to just call and let us handle it directly. We thanked him for his timely report and Laura and I caught the next flight to Cape Town. We wanted to set up our trip in Cape Town and not give her a chance to slip through our fingers again.

8:00 a.m. Sunday, October 7th Hotel Grand Cairo Lobby, Cape Town S.A.

Laura and I waited in the security surveillance room on the mezzanine and watched for Sharon to walk in. Security at the airport had already alerted us that her private jet had landed and it was only a matter of minutes before she should arrive at the hotel. We did have a police detective unit following her every step from the airport arrival terminal to the hotel as well.

What was interesting was when Sharon arrived in the hotel lobby she walked directly to the Will Call/Lost Luggage suite claimed a bag and then went to the ladies room. That was when we figured she was either on to us or she was preparing for a problem. So we walked down to the parcel post office at the rear of the lobby and stationed ourselves so we would not be seen but where we could see. Along with four other plain clothes local detectives.

When Sharon finally stepped out of the ladies room and walked across the lobby to the parcel post office I got a bad feeling in the pit of my stomach. Laura was stationed inside the post office seated behind the manager's desk near the front counter and we had a plain clothes local detective acting as if he was the office clerk. I was literally standing with my back to the post office door looking in a wall sized mirror at the door next to another local detective who was reading a newspaper and watching the front door.

Sharon walked into the post office and put her pocketbook up on the front desk and handed the clerk her ticket. The clerk walked in the back and returned with the package and sat it on the desk. Then as the normal procedure called for, he asked her for I.D. Sharon reached down inside her pocketbook with one hand and with the other pulled a s&w .38 out from under her blouse. Then she said, "Hand the package over or I will be the last person you ever see."

The detective looked at her strangely and as Laura processed what she heard Sharon say, Sharon shot the man in cold blood and was now aiming at Laura whom she recognized when see looked up from reading her newspaper.

Sharon pointed at Laura I dropped my newspaper and turned around and the detective standing behind me pulled his weapon and shouted "Police drop your weapon." By now after the first shot there was complete chaos in the lobby and I could no longer get a clear shot off. Sharon looked away towards the voice that spoke for just a second and that was all Marshal Laura needed to gain the advantage. She dropped down behind the desk she was seated at and draw her weapon by then Sharon was looking back towards her and then she fired off another round. The detective standing in front of me moved to the right towards the doorway and kneeled down as he fired three shots point blank at Sharon. I moved to the left with the full wall plate glass window between me and Sharon and I fired two burst of two shots hitting her in the upper left arm and the upper left hip. I could see where the other detective's bullets

U.S. Marshal Harry Bailey and the Case of the Deadly Psychologist

had hit her one in the lower back and the other in the upper right shoulder. She hit the floor before Laura could get a shot off.

When Sharon hit the floor I guess I thought it was all over but I was wrong. She was still alive although barely and our arrest was now in a deep dark hole called who has jurisdiction. While we had a valid international arrest warrant and had followed all of the protocols now one of their officers was dead. We had seven bodies on her and they had one but she was on their soil and we needed her to heal well enough to take her home, this was now an international mess.

When the U.S. Consulate finished sighting case law all that was left was waiting the eight weeks for Sharon to heal and us to bring her back. It took 8 weeks for a final agreement to be reached to let her return to the U.S. Neither Laura nor I realized that while Sharon was in Cape Town earlier she filed for citizenship in as a South African claiming that her father was native. Most of the eight week delay was centered on the government proving or disproving that statement which was actually true but when he gave up his citizenship before Laura's birth in the U.S. and took on U.S. citizenship she lost all rights as a foreign national.

We brought Sharon back on a air force medical evacuation plain a C-121A and held her in the medical ward at Riker's Island for about 30 days before her trial started.

9:15 a.m. Monday, December 15th, New York County Superior Court Part 15, Judge Gerald Carter Court

U.S. Marshal Harry Bailey and the Case of the Deadly Psychologist

U.S. Attorney April Montgomery was sitting on a bench outside the court room when Laura and I walked up. I asked her how she thought things were going and she said, "Things could not be going any worse if I just failed to show up for the last 10 days, where have you two been?"

I answered and said, "We have other cases you know and we just could not get away. To tell you the truth we are both working on 4 hours sleep after a hour long gun battle last night and a two hour standoff, not to mention the paperwork afterwards. You know we would have been here from day one. What's going on?"

Montgomery responded, "Your suspect has been representing herself from day one and she has been kicking my behind from the opening argument. I have managed to recover but as far as I can see at best we are neck and neck with the jury. As a psychologist she really knows how to manipulate the jury's perspective of the events. Much to my surprise Judge Carter has given her more leeway then even I expected and she is just running with it. She has managed to challenge every piece of evidence right down to the weapons used and the counterfeit money planted in your safe deposit box. This case is coming down to her word against ours."

Montgomery continued and said, "What we have to do now is trip her up. Let her ego take her all the way on a limb and then show what kind of a manipulator she really is. Harry this is going to rest on your testimony. All you have to do is answer my questions directly, just keep your answers short and sweet and to the point. When she cross examines make her feel that you are her friend, that you are on her side. I'll keep the record narrow and stop her from embellishing her points. Then when I redirect, throw her to the wolves give the whole story every detail. I want to see her crash and burn. I think she will snap and the jury will see her for the lying manipulator she is and more. Are we clear, Harry?"

10:15 a.m. Judge Gerald Carter Court

Seated at the prosecutors table Attorney Montgomery stood and said, "Your honor the People call Marshal Harry Bailey to the stand."

After I was sworn in and seated Attorney Montgomery walked up to me and stood right in front of me partially blocking Dr. Romani view and said, "Do you know the defendant?"

I responded and said, "Yes."

Then she said, "How do you know the defendant?"

I said, "I arrested her for attempted murder of my partner, fleeing prosecution, passing counterfeit bills in both the U.S., Canada, and South Africa. Kidnapping a federal law enforcement officer, kidnapping, assault, assault with a deadly weapon, murder for hire 2 counts, murder for hire of law enforcement personnel 2 counts, murder in the first degree, attempted murder of peace officer for hire…"

Montgomery interrupted me and said, "We get the picture. When you arrested the defendant were did it take place?"

I responded and said, "Cape Town South Africa in a hotel

U.S. Marshal Harry Bailey and the Case of the Deadly Psychologist

lobby."

Then Montgomery said, "Under what circumstances was the arrest effectuated?"

I said, "Under extreme circumstances, the defendant was in the process of retrieving a parcel shipped to her name from the U.S. which we believed to be the remainder of the counterfeit bills she had been proffering, when she summarily shot and killed a undercover officer of the South African Police Department for no apparent reason. She was told to drop her weapon by another South African Policemen and when she did not respond and began to draw down on my partner the officer and I fired, wounding her and then arresting her."

Then Montgomery said, "Now Marshal Bailey to the best of your recollection can you tell this court if at anytime the defendant denied any of the charges level against her?"

I responded, "She never once denied the charges."

Montgomery said, "When she was read her rights did she ever deny the charges being brought against her?"

I responded and said, "On which occasion are you referring to counselor? I personally read her, her rights on several different occasions, three of which were in Johannesburg during the initial arrest, the extradition proceedings and the departure from South Africa to Riker's Island."

Montgomery continued and said, "Now Marshal Bailey tell us, of all the charges leveled against the defendant which one or ones do you have personal knowledge of her committing if any?"

I responded and said, "When she broke into my apartment tased me, tied me and threaten to kill me if I didn't give her all of the under cover money I had left from the sting our office played on her and her associate and co-conspirator in a financial fraud case the State Banking Department had asked us to conduct."

Then Montgomery said, "Please tell the court what happened."

I went over minute by minute of the kidnapping ordeal and Dr. Romani just sat there and listened. When I finished Montgomery showed photo's of the scars from the taser to the jury.

Then Montgomery said, "No further questions your honor."

Judge Carter responded and said, "Dr. Romani your witness."

Sharon stood up and straightened her dark blue suit jacket as she walked over to the witness stand where I sat. When she got to me she positioned herself in between me and Attorney Montgomery. When she was satisfied of her position she began speaking by saying:, "Marshal Bailey is that your name?"

I responded "Yes."

Then she said, "Haven't you been called Harry Bailey as well? Even while you were actively working as a U.S. Marshal?"

Attorney Montgomery stood up and said, "Objection Your Honor, relevance."

U.S. Marshal Harry Bailey and the Case of the Deadly Psychologist

Judge Carter looked at Sharon and she said, "Goes to credibility your honor."

Then Attorney Montgomery said, "People vs. Kantor police can use deception when investigating potential suspects."

Sharon said, "If law enforcement can use deception what is to stop suspects who realize they are being investigated from using deception as well?"

Attorney Montgomery responded and said, "Mote point your honor counsel has no credible case law to support her theory."

Judge Carter spoke and said, "Sustained, the jury will disregard the last question, move on Dr. Romani."

Sharon went on and said, "Marshal Bailey is it standard police procedure for a officer of the law to seduce suspects into trusting them in order to use them for their benefit later on?"

Attorney Montgomery stood again and said, "Objection Your Honor."

Judge Carter looked at Dr. Romani and said, "How is this question different from the last?"

Sharon responded and said, "I lie about identify can be countered through public investigation but a campaign to endear a suspect through a promise of love is different."

Judge Carter thought for a moment and then he said, "You can answer that. I'll give you a little leeway but be careful."

Dr. Romani said, "Thanks your honor. Now Marshal Bailey is

that a part of standard police procedure?"

I responded, "No. It isn't but sometimes personal emotions get confused with the mission but you have to work that out on your own."

Then Dr. Romani said, "Did you attempt to seduce me Marshal Bailey?"

I responded, "No, but you tried to seduce me."

Now leaning over the witness stand Dr. Romani said, "What makes you think I tried to seduce you Marshal Bailey?"

I responded and said, "You didn't have to try very hard, I mean look at you. You are beautiful, smart, and rich at that time who could resist you?"

Dr. Romani stood up and stepped back from the witness stand and turned to the jury and said, "And what would you have done to secure my affections Marshal Bailey? Would you have slept with me? Would you have moved in with me? Would you have married me?"

Judge Carter looked at Attorney Montgomery and said, "Counselor?"

Attorney Montgomery just put her head down and said nothing.

Then Judge Carter said, "I think this line of questioning has gone far enough Dr. Romani, please move on."

Then Dr. Romani said, "Let's focus on the so-called kidnapping

U.S. Marshal Harry Bailey and the Case of the Deadly Psychologist

incident. Tell is Marshal were you really in fear of your life?"

I said, "Yes."

Then Sharon said, "You said you were restrained. How long were you restrained?"

I said, "For hours. I was tied to a kitchen chair over night and left in the middle of my living room while you plotted your next move."

Then Sharon said, "You're a big strong man, did you try to get loose from the restraints? Didn't you have to use the rest room at any point? How could I have kept you from doing that?"

I said, "You had me tied up with duck tape I could get loose."

Then she said, "Did you need to use the rest room during this overnight ordeal as you say?"

I responded and said, "I needed to go and I did right where I was tied up at, in the middle of the living room."

Sharon said, "Did the mess get cleaned up? Where you r clothes changed? Did you eat?"

I said, "Yes, but..."

And she said, "No more questions your honor." And she walked back to her seat and sat down.

Then Attorney Montgomery stood up and said, "Redirect your honor?"

RUTHLESS

Judge Carter nodded in agreement.

This time Attorney Montgomery stood just to the right of the witness box giving Dr. Romani a direct eye view of me as I responded to the questions she asked.

Attorney Montgomery said, Marshal Bailey did you ever willing or seduce Dr. Romani for any reason?"

I responded, "No."

Attorney Montgomery continued and said, "Marshal Bailey did you ever have romantic feelings for Dr. Romani of any kind?"

I looked directly at Sharon and said, "No." I could see she was hurt deeply at what I said, but it was the truth.

Then Attorney Montgomery said, "Marshal Bailey please tell the court how you felt when Dr. Romani attempted to seduce you the first time."

I said, "The first time was at a Starbucks in midtown I believe. I can't say she tried to seduce me but she definitely became flirtatious."

Then Attorney Montgomery said, "How did that make you feel?"

I spoke and said, "I felt uncomfortable un at ease, cheap, as if I needed a shower."

Then Attorney Montgomery said, "What were your thoughts?"

I said, "I was repulsed, disguised a common theft in my mind at

U.S. Marshal Harry Bailey and the Case of the Deadly Psychologist

that time, was making moves on me. I was sick to my stomach. I almost quiet the service."

Judge Carter spoke and said, "Ok Counselor we have had enough of that, move on."

Attorney Montgomery gestured okay and then said, "Talk to the jury about the next time the defendant attempted to garner your sexual interest in her."

I said, "That would be when I was in her downtown apartment. She was dressed in a negligee. She invited me to her apartment under the pretense she had some important information when all she wanted to do was have sex with me but not even right then she wanted to get me to return to her home out on long Island to do it there the next evening. It was all a rose, she had invited me to someone else's house and unbeknownst to me she had planned to have me killed there."

Then Attorney Montgomery said, "And please tell the court how did this encounter make you feel?"

I responded and said, "I can not put it into words, the case was coming together but we were in need of her continued cooperation at that time so I was caught between a rock and a hard place and I was mortified at the prospect of having to..."

That was when Judge Carter cut my testimony off. Everyone could see Dr. Romani sunk in her chair with tears in her eyes and flush in the face and neck areas.

Then Dr. Romani stood up and said, "I came to this court for justice not to be humiliated. It is shameful that the prosecution can attach me on every other area of my life but the facts of this case. From the being without help from counsel this prosecutor has attached my character, my integrity and now my sense of self worth as a woman, shame on you."

She continued on and said, "As God is my witness I do not deserve to be treated like this in a public court room. I am a learned professional, I work with people who have all kinds of mental illnesses to help them become productive members of society. No one should be treated like this. It is as if you have you case. Where is the evidence? You have none. And you have none because I left none. You thought, you think you are smarter than me? Well you are all wrong. I am the smart one, I am the pretty one, I am the sexy one, me not you. Not none of you, me and me alone. I out smarted Stephen Hamilton out of millions of dollars, not thousands, not hundreds of thousands but millions. A man who was supposed to be so brilliant was just that dumb and gullible. I seduced him at will. He was putty in my hands. You Marshal Bailey I could have had you at anytime you were like a child's toy with me. All I had to do was close my hand and I would have had your heart in it. You wanted me. You wanted me so bad you could taste it. But I wasn't ready for you to have me."

She continued and said, "You accuse me of murdering what two, three four people? Two, three four cops? I did it and I got away with it. But I played fair not under the table. I didn't bring people in to hurt your feelings as if you had none. I proved my case by the book. A book you studied I must say. Not one you read last night, like me. This system is supposed to be fair, not unfair. Even sided not one sided."

A stunned Judge Carter looked over the bench at Dr. Romani and said, "We are going to recess until after lunch I suggest you speak with your attorney about what just happened."

3:00 p.m. Judge Carters Chambers

Seated in front of Judge Carters desk was Attorney Montgomery, Dr. Romani and her counselor. Behind them stood the Judges Court Clerk, the Court stenographer, the Bailiff, Marshal Laura and myself. We had been summon to his chambers immediately after closing arguments had been heard and the Judge telling the Jury that he would probably charge them and give them the case to deliberate on first thing in the morning.

When Judge Carter walked in he took off his robe and sat down behind his desk. It was easy to see that he was not in a good mood. Matter a fact everyone could see how angry he was as he rolled up his sleeves and prepared to speak.

Finally Judge Carter spoke and said, "We have a problem. I have been contacted by a credible individual who tells me that they have evidence that you Dr. Romani killed your brother Donald Romani."

Sharon said, "That is not true your honor, I am poise to redeem my good name why would I jeopardize that by not disclosing every piece of evidence I was aware of?"

This informant tells us, both my Clerk and I, that they have both audio and video tape supporting their allegation. Now before I declare a mistrial and we have to start this whole circus all over again I want you two Marshal's to look into this and get back to me before court tomorrow morning. Is that understood?"

Marshal Laura and I both said, "Yes sir." Then he cleared the room except for his Clerk and Laura and I.

Judge Carter handed me a piece of paper with an address on it and a name, Cindy. The address was 79-18 Beach 28th Street, Rockaway Beach New York.

We took a car together to visit this Cindy, when we got there it was about 5:15 p.m. in the evening. The house was a neat and rather large bungalow backed up to the bay with a very nice view of it. Cindy a pretty young redhead was carrying a infant when she opened the door and let us in.

We introduced ourselves and Cindy showed us to the back porch and where we sat and began to talk about her conversation with Judge Carter and his Clerk as she discreetly breast feed her baby girl.

Cindy said, she had undeniable proof that Dr. Romani had killed her brother and she would be willing to turn it over to us in exchange for her daughter's inheritance.

I told her that we were in no position to negotiate an inheritance in exchange for evidence of a criminal act but maybe if she helped us better understand what she had to offer and what it was she believed was the inheritance she was talking about maybe we could be of help.

Cindy pushed a laptop computer over to us that was lying on a

U.S. Marshal Harry Bailey and the Case of the Deadly Psychologist

coffee table and said, "Open it and look."

Laura and I opened the laptop and turned it on. When it booted up Cindy told us to click on the security camera icon. When that loaded it we could see that it was a home security monitoring set of an apartments living and kitchen area. Cindy pointed us to the archive files for the date of Sunday, September 17th at 8:45 p.m. and loaded it for us to see. What we saw was Dr. Romani act and murder of her brother Donald live and in living color, from start to finish.

When the clip finished I said, "How long have you had this?"

Cindy said, "I got the laptop released to me last week and when I finished going through it this was the last file I saw. Donald and I were engaged to be married. The wedding was to be scheduled after the baby came home. Melissa was born on September 16th and he saw her for the first time on the 17th the day he was murdered." Cindy began to weep so went into the kitchen and got some tissues then returned and laid the baby down in a bassinette next to her and started to speak again.

Cindy said, "I retrieved the laptop because I knew Donald had put away some money for the wedding and the baby and his savings. He told me all about what his boss was being accused of doing. He said he was going to finish helping his sister get situated and then we would be free from that whole business and we could get married and live happily ever after. I know Donald and how he was and if thee was any proof of what he had set aside for baby Melissa it would be on his laptop. He kept everything on it. Judge Carters Court Clerk told me how I could get access to the laptop and by the time all of the paperwork went through I was able to pick it late last week. That was when I found that file and I called the Judge yesterday and went to see him at lunch today. He told me he would get back to me after court."

I asked her to tell us more about this inheritance she had expected for the baby and she said, "Donald has a file on the laptop's desk top screen named 'Savings'. In it are jpeg of purchase receipts for barer bonds and CD's he had in a safe deposit box. You know as a back up. I don't have the actual documents but I am sure they are somewhere safe in his apartment. Well they probably were safe there until the Super cleaned it out. That money should go to Melissa she is his only heir."

I asked her if Donald had acknowledged that the baby was his and she said, yes he signed the birth certificate and then she handed me an official copy of it.

I asked Cindy if she would allow us to take the laptop and show it to Judge Carter and have our lab techs see if they could verify the savings file information and get back to her with the courts decision and she said fine.

2:15 p.m. Wednesday, December 17th, New York County Superior Court Part 15, Judge Gerald Carter Court

When the jury marched in after being out for 3 hours you could hear a pin drop. Once they were seated the Court Officer handed the Judge their decision and then sent back so they could read it. Then the Judge said, "Has the Jury reached a decision?"

The Jury Foremen stood up and said, "Yes; Your Honor we have."

Judge Carter said, "What say you?"

The Jury Foremen said, "We find the defendant Dr. Sharon Romani guilty as charged on all counts."

Then Judge Carter thanked the Jury for their service and dismissed them. Then he said, "In the interest of justice sentencing will be held one week from today."

10:30 a.m. Wednesday, December 24th, New York County Superior Court Part 15, Judge Gerald Carter Court Room-Sentencing Hearing

This time Dr. Romani was brought in wearing hand and ankle chains an orange jump suit and white hospital slippers. Her hair was slightly disheveled and she didn't have on any make up but she kept her head up.

Judge Carter walked into the court room and sat on the bench while everyone stood. Then he said, "You all maybe seated. ...Will the defendant please rise?"

Then he made a brief comment about the fairest of the legal system and said, "In the interest of fairness to those who died so you could live the life you decided was most appropriate for you to live I sentence you to 50 years to life without the possibility for parole for the death of Donald Romani, and 50 years to Life without the possibility for parole for the death of

RUTHLESS

Alex Winfrey, and 50 years to Life without the possibility of parole for the death of Mark Reese. All three sentences are to run consecutively. Additionally I sentence you to 100 years to life for the deaths of Peace Officers Raymond Thomas and Glenn Beck. These sentences are to run consecutively as well. In the matter of Kidnapping a Peace Officer and holding them against the will while in the line of duty I sentence you to death by hanging to be carried out as determined by the Correctional Facility Warden so designated by the Department of Corrections of the State of New York not later than December 24th 2030. For the crime of passing counterfeit currency inside the borders of the United States I sentence you to 25 years to Life. And finally for Securities fraud and tax evasion I sentence you to 150 years to life without the possibility of parole. May God have mercy on your soul. This case is adjourned."

The End

U.S. Marshal Harry Bailey and the Case of the Deadly Psychologist

EPILOGUE

11:30 a.m. Wednesday, December 24th, New York County Superior Court Part 15, Judge Gerald Carter Court Room-Sentencing Hearing

Before Judge Carter struck the gavel to close the case he said, "It is ordered that all of the Certificates of Deposits and barer bonds as noted in the case file that were confiscated from the defendant are to be turned over to the heir of the deceased Donald Romani one and only heir Melissa Romani to be placed in trust for her until age 21 and managed by the child's guardian of record her mother until such time she is of age. It is so ordered." Then he struck his gavel.

RUTHLESS

U.S. Marshal Harry Bailey and the Case of the Deadly Psychologist

LIST OF OTHER TITLES BY THIS AUTHOR INCLUDING

U.S. Marshal Harry Bailey, and the
"The Parables of Life Series"

TITLE	RELEASE DATES
1- U.S. Marshal Harry Bailey and the case of the Persistent Widow	February 2013
2- U.S. Marshal Harry Bailey and the case of the Wicked Farmers	May 2013
3- U.S. Marshal Harry Bailey and the case of the Minas	September 2013
4- U.S. Marshal Harry Bailey and the case of the Hidden Treasure	December 2013
5- U.S. Marshal Harry Bailey and the case of the Friend at Midnight	March 2014
6- U.S. Marshal Harry Bailey and the case of the Foolish Virgins	June 2014
7- U.S. Marshal Harry Bailey and the case of the Good Samaritan	December 2014
8- U.S. Marshal Harry Bailey and the case of the Four Soils	May 2015
9- U.S. Marshal Harry Bailey and the case of the Lost Coin	September 2015
10-U.S. Marshal Harry Bailey and the case of the Prodigal Son	December 2015
11- U.S. Marshal Harry Bailey and the case of the Two Debtors	March 2016
12- U.S. Marshal Harry Bailey and the case of the Two Sons	September 2016

Ask about our SPECIAL EDITION of U.S. Marshal Harry Bailey and the case of the CORPORATE KILLINGS available now! www.usmarshalharrybailey.com

Other titles: The Way Station, U.S. Marshal Harry Bailey and the Corporate Killings and The Game of Your Life, 2-1-1 Emergency, Clinical Trials, Criminal Mastermind, The Deadly Mailman, Beyond The Way Station, Part II—To Hell for the Holidays, and look out for Black Out, The APP (Click Here for Murder), Our three volume series "The Author Part 1, the Reader Part 2, and the Publisher Part 3, in 2014 and the 6 volume series U.S. Marshal Harry Bailey and the "City of Prophesy" series coming in 2015.